I0611413

TABLE OF CONTENTS

PRELUDE

What excuse do we use when we are about to do something that we know almost everyone who knew, would be totally against??? Even if the idea had an awesome benefit and short term, positive resolution... Sometimes we kick cautions ass to the wind, do stuff and worry about the consequences if they come up. Well this read tells the tale of how GOD can use his peps, to get a message out to da people. He can do whatever He wants.

This Head Coach, Sam was ready to move on with his career and knew how to proceed. He needed the woman GOD wanted him to have. This would insure his success with what he believes is his calling, to become an NFL Head Coach.

This woman Fro is hiding, so she thinks, from relationships that could become serious. She's been asking for direction from GOD, not really expecting an answer because of what she did to help someone that only she could have helped under the circumstances. She is proud and ashamed at the same time but the end result is worth it to her?

Sam is convinced and is out to convince Fro that GOD will soon start revealing His plans and many moves made, HE will approve.

Coach and Fro have supernatural powers that only a few people know about. Only one of them knows such power exist. The other is about to find out. They go on vacation by cruise ship, seven nights and eight days, to be exact.

This book is written from an epic dream and is fiction (**fiction** defined; Literature that is a work of the imagination and is not necessarily based on fact)
Its rating is GC (may Contain Graphic Content).
Names, characters, places and incidents are product of the author's imagination or are used fictitiously. The author's dream/fantasy may have been inspired in part by her own personal desires. Any resemblance to actual events or locals or persons living or dead, is entirely coincidental and are intended to give the novel a sense of reality.

All rights reserved. No part of this book may be reproduced in any form or by any means whatsoever, without obtaining prior written permission from the author. Please do not copy this novel in its entirety. It is being self published and need all sales proceeds to fund the further distribution of this novel as a whole.
For information contact; **wholepkg_fro@cox.net**

Copyright @ 2013 The Whole Package by Frozine Boaz
ISBN 13: 978-0-9986303-0-4
ISBN: eBook pending
LCCN: 2017901234

Cover design: **covers_fro@cox.net**
Cover photograph: FSM/CCM
Photographs are sole property of FSM
This novel is being presented to you by divine providence.

First Printing May 2014
Manufactured in the USA
Printed in the USA by Lulu, Inc. of Raleigh, NC 23462

The Whole Package

by

Frozine Slater-Morrow

They both leave together knowing they won't be the same when they return. Secrets are revealed that makes it hard for Fro to ignore or deny. When she discovers and is finally convinced she is walking in her calling too, she decides to let Sam Maxwell, Head Coach of UVA Football team into her life. Together they are powerful. Apart they have power.

There are many twist and turns when Coach takes advantage and uses the cruise to attend business meetings also.

She also meets his family whom are unique in themselves. Coach Max encourages Fro to be herself and discovers he likes who she is and is becoming in front of his eyes. Neither of them can resist the other. Their lives are colliding. Is Fro ready to give up her controlling ways to be more humble? Does Sam become an NFL Coach or will he walk in Fro's calling?

This story could belong to anyone. Man or woman regardless of nationality or socioeconomics. Everyone has an idea in their minds of their ultimate love affair. Sometimes you dream about it and money doesn't matter. Who you know matters. Allowing you the pleasure of getting to know yourself is the ultimate high.

GOD will judge the wheat and the tare in the end, not us! We really do have to ride the roads of this life until the wheels fall off.

This tale is actually a Dream that is pinned to paper. It was never planned for it to be spoken out loud.

Yours Truly, Frozine

No matter what our plans are...
GOD *plants us where* ***HE*** *wants us to be...*
When ***HE*** *wants us to be there and*
chooses the road ***HE*** *wants us to take.*

The EXCUSE

Agony is the only way to describe what
I <u>felt</u> when presented with this quandary.
He needed a chance to get through this,
unbroken. <u>I believed</u> I was capable of
handling this but with so many other things on
my plate this was hard to ignore.
<u>I just knew</u> if I convinced myself this was for
a good cause and in no way was a permanent
solution, my actions would be <u>justified</u>. My
final answer was, for once in my life and
maybe only once...
*I am going to allow, I felt, I believed, I
just knew and justified win.*
The goal would be I help you by encouraging
and protecting you when necessary. You have
to do the work. If you do your part, I will do
mine. You and I will benefit even if it's not a
balanced measure. The only requirement I
have is total anonymity.

If ever asked your answer has to always be No!!
Ride or Die!! No backsies!!
The benefit for me would be the ability to get
away, relax and keep fun in my life, for me. If
I always focus on someone else, I can easily
lose myself, if only for a short time.
As a single parent with a school aged child
that I am active with, I sometimes need away
time, just to keep focused and regain my
energy. Besides I have no interest in a
relationship right now.
*Is this how people start out on a journey,
without an exit strategy?*
Anyway, if I can help get him past the worst,
until he can handle things on his own, it is
worth it.

If I can help

It's been **a year** now. My first visit was the 3rd month of school. I made it a point to make sure I was on the will call list for the home football games and a few away games. I always traveled alone, that way no one could keep tabs on me but me. Some friends wanted to travel to the college for the games too but they couldn't ride with me. I told them I may have to leave at anytime even if they weren't ready. No one wanted to be inconvenienced or have to gauge their plans around me. This is a tactic I used to be able to come and go whenever I wanted to. The two hotels I used were near the college. I checked in on Friday night and out on Sunday morning.

Cee would come by my room before curfew. He brought his books and a change of clothes. We talked a while about what was happening with him, his friends, teachers and new people he met. He told me he was enjoying the single shower privilege. He's now not embarrassed by the other guys looking at him too long when he took public showers. Cee had a large penis. Larger than his teammates who he associated with everyday.

His roommate accidentally saw him and told him a girl will accuse him of rape if he tried to have sex with her with that massive muscle.

Cee was angry a lot at first and wanted to quit, go home and get a job at Lowe's or Home Depot. He played football extremely well and loved it. His moves seemed effortless. He deserved a chance to excel in his gift but this held him back. I told Frank, his coach, the immediate solution was to allow him to shower in the coach shower. This wasn't a real big deal. He would use the excuse that he has a birth defect and didn't want to gross them out, if any one demanded a reason. They would be more likely to feel sorry for him if they thought it was small in size as opposed to them feeling threatened by his actual size. Cee was doing better in school after this. He was of course a young man and no matter what size he was he needed relief some time. That is how this all started.

During my first visit he asked me to let him have sex with me so he wouldn't be so horny all the time. He said this feeling was almost a burden. He was afraid to act because he could kiss football goodbye and he would catch a criminal charge. There lies the quandary.

After careful thought I entered into an agreement with him. I would have sex with him all home games and a few away games. All rules applied as stated earlier. No condoms, so we had to know the other was committed. We both brought out our medical reports showing each was free from STD's and HIV. Then it started. Cee and I had sex twice during the home games and once during away games. We also had sex at the end of football season, including before the Super Bowl. The only time this didn't happen is when someone was sick. So I was having sex 10 times a year. I wouldn't allow Cee to see me or have sex when it wasn't football season. He would sometimes call me late asking for a quickie but I refused. I didn't want him to fall in love with me, because I had no plans of falling in love with him. He was young enough to be my son, I wasn't crossing that line. Imagine me, having ethics during all this.

Cee would get excited when he knew we were about to have a visit. The sex would be long and hard. He was really horny the first time and it showed. We would study and I read his books to him while he took notes. This was so he would know the lesson and not have to guess.

He liked and excelled using this learning method. I was happy to see him applying himself in his classes. I and he knew he would need good grades to make it. He had to know and retain the information. He was good and he kept getting better.

We had sex first during our meetings and spent the rest of the time allotted to open the curtains, while we studied. We'd be up until 1 am sometimes, longer. After the game and the players talk from the coach, I would wait at the gate of the gym for him or he would walk over to my hotel.

I once met the head coach after a game. I didn't say anything to him or get close to him. Cee told me word on the street was that coach was a whore. A lot of women were always after him. I certainly didn't have time for that drama so I kept my distance. I would also bring Cee food that I cooked and knew he liked. I knew he shared it because I would never bring any back. Cee was indeed large and I often wondered, at first, why he wasn't too large for me to handle.

Initially he was nervous and afraid of hurting me but when he found out it didn't hurt, he got his in. I let him.

He would pick me up, hold me up against the wall and pump it all the way up. I think that was his favorite position.

It has worked out well this season. Cee is progressing on the team and in school. I was reaping the benefit of helping keep him in school and I get rest and relaxation.

The **2nd year** ended in a stamina game. He was becoming confident in his abilities to get a certain reaction during sex. I believe I'm pretty good at control but he has left me wondering, who is really the gate keeper. A few times I had to run from him for real. He was trying to snatch me up! I had to have the original talk with him again to refresh his memory of our rules that he agreed to.

I also brought up the fact that he's progressing well and could actually accomplish good things for the future. I will be sharing this future with him, no matter what. I told him he should continue seeking his soul mate because it wasn't me. He chilled after that. He knew I was right. He didn't want to jeopardize having none as opposed to getting some temporarily, 10 times a year.

When Cee went for his checkup I went with him. He gave permission for me to be there. We asked about the size of his penis and the problems it causes. The Dr. must have been sent from GOD because he had information Cee could use. He said there is a group of men with the same issue. They even have meetings and share helpful information for others in their same position.

Cee and I both were happy to hear this. It can be scary when you seem to be the odd one. It's nice to know he/we are not alone. The Dr. asked us a question that even I wasn't sure how to answer. He asked Cee if I was helping him in this area of his life. Cee answered, 'No, but it's not for the lack of trying'. I smiled without answering.

The Dr. said, 'that's too bad, because that would actually help Cee be more stable and focused on school as opposed to sex or the fact that he can't have sex normally without a risk. He is after all a healthy male otherwise.'

I went to the home games with the same ritual but I stopped going to the away games so I could spent more time with my daughter. Cee was still doing great in class and on the football field.

However, we were not on the same page. He wants to make love with me. I don't want to do that. Well, I stepped out there and let this young man have me.

He brought it and a few other things fell in line. He took it as we're in love instead of we're in luck, that time. He called me often and was a little jealous. These were games I didn't play anymore. I told him he had to find out if there's a list of women who can handle men his size, besides me. We made love, at least five times. I have to do something to help this phase, along.

I called the Dr. and told him Cee needed a list of meetings/dates to find a suitable match for himself, someone his age with a common personal profile to each other. Race not a factor.

He said this is strictly confidential and if I ever say one word about it, my life will be ruined. I figured I could handle any secret like that since it involved Cee. I felt responsible for him and wouldn't let anyone take advantage of him.

Once or twice he cancelled our meeting. He said he had plans with his school friends. I was so happy to hear this. He was being weaned from me and it felt great.

Look at that, an exit strategy I just used to help everything along. That wasn't in my plan but was right on time.

Cee was finishing his 2nd year of college on time and in good shape. He had minimal injuries because coach taught them how to work to their full potential and techniques for healing. Coach Max was a good man for the team. I was glad he took time with Cee. He knew Cee would be a beast if guided properly.

I've been feeling like we are in transition right now. A transition I've been waiting for. Cee is getting closer to me and he needs to let go. I had to admit he was wearing me down. It would be easy to love him because I already did love him. It's just this love was not in love. I was on a different level than Cee. He would probably be on my level one day but it didn't have to be now. I knew this was my fault. Cee didn't care about that. He was ready to love a woman for real and add his emotions and feelings. I wasn't the woman who could handle that.

GOD had to be preparing me for something. When you go through unusual things and the answer goes to GOD, you might as well say Thanks for being used, in His plan.

So now that I knew GOD took over my plan I was readying myself for the ride.

We still ended this year with 10 sessions. I was very good with holding the line. I failed during the Spring Break. He got a room at the beach and invited me. I felt frisky so I went. He jumped me right away. He didn't give me time to say no at all.

He knew this was it for this year so he went there. He spent 20 minutes looking for my spot that I had no idea I had. He didn't find it or it took more time then he had, to find it. That is a lesson for another day.

This was the 3rd **year** I was hoping it was the last for Cee and I and the arrangement we had entered into. He worked in the gym all summer. He was bulked up now. He had a lot of confidence and I could tell he was wiser too. He must have had a long talk with GOD. I know I had. My husband had only been gone a year when I called myself helping Cee. Even though the result of the plan was successful, the exit was not so smooth. During our first connection of this year, he wanted to try a new position and he wanted to change it to study 1st and sex afterwards.

We reviewed his course schedule. I saw where I could help and with which subject he had to get other help. We would sit on the hotel balcony and spread papers around and worked hard until he got it. I was so proud of him and almost felt sorry that he was in this position with his large penis.

After we finished studying, we ate and took showers for the love making that I tried to keep to only sex. He was beginning to explore my body and wanted to know what I liked. He could make me come just sucking my breast. This gave him enough juice to lay the rod all the way down. Straight sex had gotten boring for both of us so I allowed him to try new things as long as there was no anal penetration. He came faster when I let him have oral sex. So I pushed the oral sex first. This worked a few times but soon he caught on and wanted to control the tempo. He screwed me in many positions and showed me a few things about his power and ability to make me come at will. He found my spot. I tried to pretend he didn't but he leaned on it until I moaned and cried out for him to stop. My body tightened up when his massive penis brushed it.

Whenever I tried to reposition myself he found one of his new positions and adjusted his position. He pushed in and out and side to side until I moaned loudly. He felt my body react then positioned himself to absorb the blow and rode it out until he came with me. He was so happy to be able to have sex freely without the threat of jail time. But something was happening.

He was touching me more tenderly and he kissed me more often which made me more comfortable. He was stronger now so he took delight in holding me up in the air and sucking my nipples with such passion, juice would drip on the floor, then he would lay me on the bed face down, get on his knees and taste my soft spot until I came again then he screwed me on the floor, in the tub, on the chair, on top of the sink, up against the wall and the bed. I was beginning to feel tired.

Whomever he ended up with would certainly have to be able to match his energy. This went on for the first half of the season. Then he skipped a few times after we studied. I was happy with this decision.

He said he met a girl but wasn't sure about her yet. He was taking it slow.

The last time we were together, we kind of knew it would be the last time. He forced me to keep it real and I allowed myself to feel what he gave. If I were 30 years younger I would have snatched him up but that was certainly not an option now.

I liked the total control style he used and knew I would miss him but as long as he was doing well in school and met a girl who was compatible in the area that matters, I was good.

One day Cee will be a great football player with his degree, which will take him to another level. He will know what it means to really help others. Maybe he will be a coach. Whatever his plans were I would always encourage him, with no expectation.

Even though I would deny it, I pray he doesn't discuss our intimate relationship.

I went as far as asking GOD, in prayer, to take away or hide the sexual memories from Cee and myself. Was hoping GOD heard me.

It is beginning to feel like I'm never going to find a partner. A regular man won't do. I'm tired of waiting and have decided for myself, that part of my life is dead, and if it isn't I will kill it. A thought entered me. "Who was I, to make any attempt, to kill GOD's plan?"

I'm not qualified to do this. I will proceed in life with caution, when it comes to relationships with men.

I am 50 years old and without cover. Lots of women find themselves here every day but I never thought I would be counted in this statistic. I already know how to do a lot of things well, have an ability to win friends and influence people.

I'm not a model but I'm in great physical condition. Men approach me with interest, everyday. I don't wear makeup much and 4inch heels are not my friend.

Even though I am debt free now, I am not encouraged because I am yet unfulfilled. Something is missing in my life and it has nothing to do with money.

Would be nice if 3seats is more than a dream, at least I could be doing something for The Father that mattered.

GOD, if it's not asking too much, please send me, someone special, that needs me, to LOVE!

We Met

This day had to come one day. I am happy for him and his girl. She is still with him so she must know his story by now. He told me she was the one so I have to believe she can handle him as he is. I'm also sad to be losing our special friendship. Even though it is a secret, now, as it has been all along. I am happy I could help him and enjoy the benefits for these past three years. It was nice hiding out every other weekend and to tell the truth I will miss it and him but he has to live his life and it can't be with me.

So many thoughts are running through my head right now. Practice was over. Cee came by my hotel room to speak and bring Antonia to meet me. He was excited for my approval of her, I could tell in his voice and the way he did not touch me. She was quiet, almost seemed humble when I shook her hand. I glanced into her dark eyes and said, 'You are her?' She said, "Yes".

I smiled at her confidence and looked at Cee. He searched my face for approval. I smiled at him and said, "Ok". I could hear him breathe deep.

When he grabbed her hand and said"Let's go",
my heart ached a little because I knew it was
over.

He turned to me and said, "Some of the coaches
are gathering for a drink down by the tennis
courts you should go."

This was a first after 3 years of suggesting I
stay away from them. Whores, is what he called
them. I looked away and pretended I had been
thinking of something else. I said, "I may go to
say goodbye for the season". He said, "That's
what's up".

I didn't want to leave tonight and with no plans
and no friend to kill the time with, maybe having
a beer or two with the coaches would be
entertaining, if nothing else.

As they left my room, a bit of loneliness started
filling inside me.

It was too late to drive back home tonight,
besides the room was paid for. I might as well
let my hair down and join the assistant coaches
for a beer.

I grabbed my back pack and left the hotel for
the five minute ride over to the campus tennis
courts. The closest park was up the hill on a
side street. I decided to park there so I would
have a chance to talk my nervous stomach down.

I could see the picnic tables beside the courts. There appeared to be a few people, mostly men, standing around talking. I couldn't hear what they were saying which made me feel better. I could blend into their midst without bringing attention to myself since I was alone.

I recognized the defense coach right away. When I was close enough to him, he called me over. "What's up Fro? Have a beer." I smiled and went to the cooler he pointed to. To my surprise there was a Dos Equis sitting on top. I smiled and grabbed it.

Wow, they had a few of the beer I like. 'What are those odds?', I wondered. They had pulled a few tables together so there was enough room without sitting so close to each other.

There was a woman already seated at the far end of the table. I recognized her from a few of the games. She was always on the sideline but not a coach or trainer. She waved at me with a smile. I waved back, but didn't sit next to her. All of the coaches present were 6ft or taller. The head coach wasn't present. I was comfortable with this since I wasn't really interested in meeting, 'the whore', as Cee had always described him.

Frank, the defensive coach knew my name from Cee sharing my cooking with him. I always came to visit Cee and brought his favorite food items. This was one way of showing him I cared.

His mom was not able to check on him because she was locked up for writing bad checks. I suppose that was one reason I didn't mind helping him.

Frank repeated my name and the others turned to see why he called me and I didn't answer. I was deep in thought, day dreaming about Cee and glad he would be okay. I jumped and said, 'Sorry! Just thinking about how good this beer is.' I lied. They laughed. We all laughed.

One of the other coaches said, 'Well, I don't believe this, Coach came. I looked up and to my right coming across the field was a tall, fit man with a nylon sweat suit, in school colors. I took the last swallow of my beer. I asked Frank if I could have another beer. He said of course, pointing to the cooler. He then turned his attention to Coach. "Which wind blew you out here?' he said. Coach smiled. I tried not to look directly at him but could barely keep my eyes off him. He was FINE! I moved back towards my seat when he noticed me.

'So who do we have here', he asked out loud.

Frank answered nervously, 'This is the lady who has been keeping Cee on track. Remember all that food you ate from Cee? This is Fro'.
He walked over and extended his hand, with a smile. We both felt the electricity. Our eyes met...My hand gripped the bottle neck of my beer in fear of dropping it. I felt warmth all through my body start to bubble up. I couldn't tell if I was nervous from finally meeting a real whore or was he a real, down to earth man, misunderstood. 'Oh GOD!' What have I gotten myself into?'
I was satisfied basking in my hearts loneliness, too scared to show me to anyone. I slowly pulled my hand from his. He smiled. 'So, you are the lady I've wanted to meet? I've always wanted to thank you for the grub.' I couldn't believe Cee shared my food I prepared for him, with Coach. 'You're welcome, I suppose'. That's all I could muster up. I took a long swig of my beer so I didn't have to say anything else.
 I sat at the table and acted as if I wasn't the stranger that I was. 'Have a brew Coach,' Frank said. Coach turned away from me and walked over to the cooler and pulled out the same beer I had. He walked back over and sat across from me.

Frank and the other coaches started laughing and talking about meeting the parents of the new players that were coming to campus in the summer. They described the hot moms they had already met and the thug dads. I laughed a little when it seemed like they were describing Cee's dad. He had always looked like a gangster to me.

Coach Sean, the offensive coach looked at Coach and said, 'Hey Coach is that fine woman still chasing you? I saw her on campus a few days ago. I believe she was looking for you.' Everyone laughed like it was some inside joke. Coach didn't laugh but shook his head, side to side. He looked straight at me.

I almost felt sorry for him because he seemed annoyed by the thought of her. I took another long swig of my beer in an attempt to not laugh and make him look away. He did not. All I could think was, 'this man is so fine, too fine to be a whore.' Wish I could have gotten to him before he chose to whore around. So sad, that the fine ones do that. What a waste. He smiled and so did I. He said, 'Man, you know I don't want that woman.'

Coach Sean shot back, 'yeah, yeah I know!

You waitin on your woman that GOD sent you. You already met her, just waitin for her to return. You have been saying that for 2 years man.'

There was music playing on a box at the end of the table. The woman that was seated next to Coach Frank got up and danced to the music, where she stood. It was a smooth oldie song. Coach Sean jumped up and caught her hand. He pulled her to the side of the tennis court, right off the grass.

There was a step stool with two steps on it. She climbed up to reach his 6'2" frame. We all laughed. Coach Frank said in a low voice, 'he beat me to it again.' Coach said, 'you can't sleep on Sean, man.'

Coach Frank turned to me and asked if I left food with Cee. I told him no, I was not staying the whole weekend. I had to go home with my daughter. Coach asked where I lived. I told him I lived in Virginia Beach, where Cee is from. We all talked a little about the many players from that area.

I said, 'too bad this college is not part of the MEAC, I have had so much fun attending.' Coach said, 'yeah, we have gone for the past few years but I never saw you.'

I laughed thinking of my past performances there. I said, 'you wouldn't have recognized my wig.' Coach swallowed hard. He laughed out loud as if I had told a joke. I was almost offended but he reached out and caught my hand. He pulled me to him from across the table. He said, 'Dance with me!'

I started pulling my hand back but he wouldn't release it. He said, 'Please!' He was no longer laughing. He looked serious almost. I got up and he released my hand. The music playing now was soulful and made you want to sway. He walked around to my side of the table. I turned and looked at Coach Frank. He waved for me to go on. I looked at Coach again. He said, 'after you.' We passed Coach Sean and the woman on the way. The woman yelled for me to use the step stool. I didn't answer or turn around. Not sure if I would take her advice.

Coach was about 6'3" and I was wearing 3" wedge sandals which made me about 5'7". My head would meet his upper chest.

When we got to the court and off the grass he said, 'stand on the stool, I won't let you fall, I want to talk to you for a minute, please.' I said okay.

The song was half finished when he came close to me and held my hand without our bodies touching.

I was happy on both accounts. I was nervous being that close to him anyway.

After all he was Head Coach of the football team and a fine man with a persistent woman pursuing him.

He chose his words very carefully. We swayed with the music.

He said, 'Fro, I believe I have seen you at the MEAC a few years ago. You took my breath away and I knew you then like I know you now. I've been looking, no, waiting for you. Let me get to know you.'

I couldn't let on that I was stunned so I calmly took a breath and held it a moment before letting it go. How do you know I am the woman you saw? I asked. He said, 'you wore a wig with curls right?' He said, 'you wore NSU colors right?' I was getting more nervous by the second. The music stopped but another song came on similar to the last. We continued to dance and sway in rhythm. I said, 'I wore something like that 2 years ago.' He said, 'I know.'

I looked at him almost eye level. He had beautiful eyes that were light in color but not gray or blue. I couldn't help but think he was attempting to try and play me and I was not having it.

Just as the thought settled inside me, he came close, very close, almost touching but not. His lips brushed mine. He kissed my air as I took a breath. I felt it but knew he had not touched me. Electricity ran through me and I released a moan. I was stunned he could provoke that from me, without my permission. He said, 'Thank You GOD,' in a low voice. The music stopped. He helped me off the step stool and we walked back over to the picnic table in silence and without looking at each other.

I didn't sit again. I told Coach Frank I was tired and ready to go back to the hotel now. He said, 'Did Coach run you off or something?' I said, 'or something.' He looked at Coach and said, 'Sam Maxwell, what have you done to my friend?'

I quickly spoke up before Coach could defend himself. I told Coach Frank it was not Coach but me. I was a little tipsy from the beer and needed to go since I was driving. He seemed okay with the answer.

He said, 'Coach, why don't you walk Fro to her car so no one bothers her. You know that woman may have seen you two dancing.' I hadn't thought of that and turned to look at Coach. He smiled. 'Of course I will,' he said. I reminded Frank that I don't play that shit with no woman, about no man, that's not mine. Not yet, is what I wanted to say, but didn't. Frank said he really wanted me to walk Coach to his car so that woman would get the message that Coach was not interested in her. He felt bad that Coach was always looking over his shoulder trying to avoid this woman. He wished the woman wanted him instead. She was very pretty. Sam laughed and reached out for my hand. I allowed him to take it and we walked back to my car. When we were far enough away not to be heard, Coach asked me if I had a boyfriend. I told him, no. He said that was good because he wanted me to become his woman. He said he didn't want Coach Frank or Coach Sean to know I was the woman on the picture. I did not believe his story but agreed. When I put my key in and started the car, he reached inside with his upper body and kissed me on the lips, very softly. He said, 'I will call you soon." I said okay although again I did not believe him.

Becoming Familiar with the Plan

It was three days since my return from my weekend college visit. Spring was here and trees were blooming. There was lots of activity going on around me, too many to be lonely but I was. My husband had been gone for 3 years now, I missed him.

The relationship with Cee was changed since he found his girl, Antonia. It was good to know he would be okay. I had spent lots of time with him making sure he knew someone really cared and made sure he got through the tough times without going to jail or getting kicked out of school. I was proud and ashamed at the same time but the end result was worth it. I had helped someone through a time in their lives that no one else could have helped.

My heart was glad but I knew no one outside of those involved would agree or understand.

I did not care what others thought now. Cee would never tell and neither would I.

That's the only way I agreed to help in the first place. My youngest child was almost a high school senior and soon I would have an empty house.

I was not looking forward to that but was looking forward to the freedom. I often consulted GOD asking what the plan for me was but have not gotten an answer or so I thought. My house was paid for and so was my car but I still felt unfulfilled. GOD had given me 3SEATS many years ago to share with the people but I had not carried it forward because I did not have the resources to develop and implement the idea and was waiting for GOD to do it or help me. I thought maybe it was my dream and not GOD's idea. Maybe HE forgot about me or I was being punished.

On Friday afternoon just after I kicked off my shoes and sat on the couch wondering what the weekend would bring, my cell phone buzzed. It was Cee. We greeted each other like real friends. He wanted me to know he was good and more confident than before. I told him I missed him but totally understood and always want the best for him. He told me he wanted the same for me. He paused for a moment, I thought he hung up or it was a dropped call. He proceeded to tell me how wrong he was for misjudging Coach. I asked him what he meant. He told me that it turned out Coach was not a whore. There were women who chased him.

He didn't want to be accused of any wrong doing so he avoided most women. I didn't tell Cee about my conversation with Coach nor did I mention the fact that he kissed me. He told me that he overheard Coach Sean say so. He also asked if he could give my number to Coach. Okay, but why would he want to do that? I thought. 'Cee honey, why would you want to give your coach my phone number?' I asked. There was a brief silence again. 'He asked me for it, I saw him today. I told him I couldn't give it to him without asking you first. He said you wouldn't mind. I told him I had to ask you first anyway.' What was this man up to? Then again I did not give him my number when I was there. I suppose he forgot to ask. I don't want to go through changes to go out with or date this man. Relaxation almost had me sleeping. My phone buzzed again. This time it was a text message. *(Hello Fro)* I didn't recognize the number. (Hello, who's this?) *(Coach Sam)* (Who is Coach Sam?) *(Stop playing with me woman)* (I don't know u) *(Not yet)* (Really, who is this?) *(Sam Maxwell)* (Where did u get my#?) *(Cee)* *(Can we talk?)* (Yes, bout what)

Just then the phone rings. The number was the same one the text came from. He flirted with me for awhile before he seemed to get serious. It was nice sparring with someone my age and similar level of intelligence. His voice was deep and sexy.

It sounded like he was lying down. I certainly was. I asked him what he wanted with me. He said he needed me, I asked why. His response was surprising to me. He said he could show me better than tell me. I smiled. Glad he couldn't see me. He laughed. It almost seemed like he could see me or read my mind. Felt a little eerie. The whole time he was talking it was hard to concentrate because I kept wondering why all of a sudden he was even talking to me. There were plenty of other women around that would love to have him, the handsome, Samuel Maxwell, Coach of UVA Football team, call them. I wondered what I did to deserve his attention. The only thing that came to me was he was playing me to pass time or maybe a bet. Who else would meet someone in a photo years before and wait to meet them again. It sounded strange to me. I just knew I was not going to make it easy for him to do whatever his plan was, to me. He would have to win me over.

I was still on leave from work. Ever since my husband passed I was still a wreck. It felt like GOD forgot me and I was supposed to be alone. My youngest was busy doing high school activities. I tried to hide the fact that I was lonely but she knew. We talked, cried and consoled each other every so often.

She worked a part time job locally but was planning to visit relatives during the summer. Sam and I talked every few days on the telephone. He always asked me questions about what I like and what I wear or don't wear. He asked if I liked sex. I told him yes but have never been totally satisfied. He said he had the same issue. He asked me if I would go on a boat cruise with him. I said maybe one day when I trusted him more.

I could pay to go on a cruise myself but was not inclined to do so right now. I wanted to tone up. Sam said I looked good to him but he understood how women felt about their bodies. I surprised him after he asked me again in May. I told him I would go if he promised to be good and not take advantage of me or make me feel self conscious about myself. He promised.

I was actually thinking maybe we could play, what happens on the ship stays on the ship. Maybe he would be able to satisfy my hunger that had been building for so long. But if he couldn't I would be stuck on a cruise ship with him. He ran with the answer given. It was several days before he called to tell me the date and ask how we would travel. I, of course suggested driving. Just in case I could not go through with it, I could stop in South Carolina and stay for a little while.

He agreed with the drive. It would give us a chance to vibe. He chose an 8 day 7 night cruise. We would take his SUV. He said he would pay for me. I told him I could pay for myself but he wouldn't hear of it. I was suspicious of his motives. But he assured me he was a gentleman and wouldn't hurt me. I took his word. Even though I was enjoying talking with Sam, I was not looking for a relationship with him. There was no one I wanted to be with right now seriously. My thoughts were that real, complete love had been hiding from me for so long, it was my turn and so far I was doing a good job at hiding. Helping Cee up at the college provided me the opportunity to hide from men my age.

I didn't want to make any commitments to anyone else if I wasn't getting what I wanted and needed out of the relationship. My desires were to meet HIM! The man I could encourage and could encourage me. My man, who would and could satisfy my sexual desires and allow me to take it to him also. There are things GOD called me to do that are too big for me and I am now wondering if GOD really gave me the dream or was it just a dream. Will I die, pregnant with this dream? Better yet, will I die unfulfilled, sexually? I don't need money or material things. I need and want the whole package.

My friends, relatives and books always talk about compromise and work. I say, I can hang if he brings it.

The next day Sam called with more questions and a few answers. He said not to worry about my hair on the cruise. He had that covered. I figured he was prepared to pay the salon to fix it. He told me not to bring too many clothes and bathing suits, he knew someone who I could get a few swim suits from on the islands. This sounded like fun already. I asked where exactly we would be stopping. He said, Jamaica, Caymans and Cozumel, the last stop would be in Key West.

I had taken this route on a previous cruise and enjoyed it. He said he knew people at every port. I figured with his position as a coach he would have traveled the islands.

It dawned on me that I didn't know very much about this man. I asked where he was born. He said Jamaica to a native woman and a white/mixed man from the States. He said his mom died when he was still in Junior High School. He lived with his Godparents and then went to stay with his father during high school. I asked was he ever married. He said he was but had been divorced for ten years. He volunteered the next answer before I asked the question. Yes, I have 2 grown children, a son and daughter. No, my ex-wife was never mistreated nor my children. He said his heart told him not to marry her but he was tired of being alone and thought they could make it but he was wrong. She could not handle him sexually nor did she try. She got pregnant the first time they attempted to have intercourse. He wasn't fully erected because she complained of pain even though she was not a virgin. She complained so often he hardly ever asked her to be with him. The next year she masturbated with him and caught his sperm in a cup.

He said he was done with her when she took a
long syringe, sucked up the sperm and inserted
it into her vagina. She left soon as she found
out she was pregnant. She told him she didn't
love him or want him touching her anymore. He
said this action shook his core.

So his father helped him by paying her in
advance what he would have to pay in child
support for 18 years. His father was a business
man and he was his only son. His father didn't
want him to be betrayed and taken for a
rollercoaster ride all of his life. He appreciated
his father for the gesture.

He didn't realize it at the time but it was the
best thing his father could have done for him.
Turns out the ex-wife told the children their
father died and threatened to tell anyone who
would listen, that he raped her if he ever tried
to contact her or the children.

He believed her and the fact that she would
press charges against him even if she did not
win, would ruin him and his ambitions.

This is the reason he has not had a real
relationship for the past 10 years. When he
tried before, it didn't go well.

Apparently the man was healthy when it came to
sex. All the women he met could not handle him.

He said he often thought he was cursed to be
so well endowed. My ears perked up!
I have been looking for this situation my entire
adult life. Don't let me find out he has been
within reach for the past two years and I didn't
know. Now that would be laughable.
As if on cue, he said, 'Fro, I believe you are my
soul mate.' I said, 'Sam, you don't know me or if
I can satisfy you. What makes you think I could
be your soul mate?' He took a deep breath
before answering me.
'I didn't tell Sean or Frank that you were the
woman in the picture I took two years ago.
They would have thought I was crazy.'
'GOD led you to me and vice versa. Don't you
believe HE has the ability to do that?
HE is who HE is you know. HE saved you for me
and vice versa. I believe it has been confirmed.
'By who?' I asked, getting and feeling defensive.
Who did Sam think he was? Who does he know
that knows me other than Cee and I knew he
wouldn't tell Sam anything about me, the little
bit he did know. Sam could hear me getting
agitated by his revelation. He quickly answered,
using my words against me. He said, 'wait baby!
You said yourself that you have been searching
for someone like me, all your life, didn't you?

If not for GOD, who else could have brought us together?' He had a point but that remained to be seen.

We have never gone on a date together, had an intimate exchange or anything physical. 'Okay, I'm sorry! You are right. I did say that. I didn't think you remembered. It's just scary because I have been purposely hiding my heart for years. I'm tired of the bullshit when it comes to relationships. I can't take another shallow or incomplete relationship. I refuse.'

'So are you calling me shallow, Fro?' We both laughed. 'No, Sam. I'm not!

Tell me, are you taking me on a cruise so I can't run or avoid you and your desire to see if I am HER?'

He said, 'Fro, you're avoiding me now. I asked you a question and you changed the subject. What's that about? You haven't realized I do listen to you and I hear what you say and what you don't say. You are something else woman but I wouldn't have you any other way.

My cousin use to say we playing Jedi's. You know, Jedi Master, Yoda? Are you playing Yoda tricks on me?'

We both laughed so hard, I almost cried. He said, 'Don't under estimate me or my abilities.

You will always be surprised.' I said, 'Ok, my bad Sam. You are not shallow. I'm just a little, no, a lot, relationship shy. I believe you are very intelligent and perceptive. You often surprise me when we are discussing things. It's like you can read my mind but it feels nice that we are on most of the same pages. Did I answer your question that time?' I smiled. He said, 'yes, okay but watch that. I'm not your average brother. You are not the average sister either, that's one of the things that interest me about you.'

He asked me to give him a chance before I make final judgment. He said he promises I will not regret giving him the opportunity to prove he is who he says he is.

I could only answer, yes okay, my brother, the Jedi Master for real. We both laughed again. Sam talked about why he wanted to cruise. He said he had not been on vacation in a long time and neither had I.

We would be away from telephones for the most part and eyes that would like to keep up with his every move. He wanted to introduce me to those he loved and that loved him. He had friends and things he wanted me to see.

He wanted me to get to know the person no one else knows with certainty. And yes we would be comfortable sleeping on the ship every night no matter where we were during the day.

He said he was prepared to go all out to convince me that we were meant for each other. I couldn't help but wonder what I had that Sam Maxwell wanted bad enough to go through this much trouble to get.

There is one week left before the cruise.

I am nervous as hell. I'm taking one suitcase with two swim suites. All my sandals are 3 inches so I won't be so short when Sam and I take photos on the ship. Even if I'm not his girlfriend I certainly want to look cute.

I will take a few extra bags so I can bring back rum cream from the Caymans.

If things don't go right with my date, I have to be prepared. My iPod has to have plenty of music it will be a long ride home. I will also have to be prepared to take a flight home.

That will be a last resort plan, just in case we run into an old flame that's not really old.

I will not go blow to blow for Sam. But if some woman puts her hands or body in my space, I will not rule out a less than positive reaction. But I will not fight over Sam.

This is crazy thinking, right before vacation. I am going to have a great vacation no matter what. I will depend on GOD to guide and protect me and my heart.

'GOD, if he is my soul mate, Thank you. I will enjoy the journey, I promise. If this is an attempt at taking total advantage of my heart, please protect me because I will not allow another man to get close to it again. AMEN.'

Sam and I spoke on the phone a few times before he came to pick me up. He seemed calmer than before. It was nice talking with him. He didn't ask me so many questions now. He would leave at noon and drive the two hours to pick me up. He asked me to be ready so we could clear rush hour traffic.
I agreed. We both agreed that no matter how this trip turned out, our lives would forever be changed.
He said he was confident that I would be his woman when he brought me back.

The Adventure Starts

My youngest was tucked away with local friends.
She hugged me tight and I her. She insisted I
have a great time. I assured her that was the
plan no matter what. She would get a call in the
middle of the week.

Here we go...Sam wore shorts above the knee.
He had really nice muscle legs with light hair on
them. He wore a button down sports shirt. His
chest hair was showing since he had the first 3
buttons open. My insides started getting hot. I
hugged him lightly then moved away quickly. He
smiled and said, 'too late to be scared now.' I
blushed. I wore a white crochet halter with
matching long skirt I had a cover crochet top
for later at night when it got cool. My cleavage
was visible and so was my medium sized butt.
My nails and toes were polished with attractive
tri-color patterns.

Even though my hair was natural, it was flat
ironed and crimped. I had on Maui Jim sun
glasses. He asked me if I was asking for
trouble dressed like that. I responded, 'I live
at the beach and I'm on vacation, this is how we
roll.' He responded, 'okay then!'

I didn't mention that I was not wearing panties because of the heat and convenience of going to rest stop bathrooms. I glanced over at him, he chuckled to himself almost as if he heard me. I asked him what was so funny. He said nothing really. Just imagining what color panties you would wear under white so you can't see your panty lines. I didn't answer. I smiled to myself thinking, 'wouldn't you want to know.'

We made it to 95 South in good time.

Now for the long ride! I drove through North Carolina then he took over until we got to Georgia. We stopped in Georgia to grab some dinner. I ate light so I wouldn't have stomach issues on the highway. When we got back on the road, I drove. Sam asked if the smell of a cigar bothered me. I asked him if the smell of a joint bothered him. We both shook our heads at the same time. I poured my ice out of my cup through the window and pulled out a joint I had wanted to smoke since we left Virginia. He pulled a half smoked cigar from his bag in the seat behind us. We opened the sun roof and began to smoke. He played a Kenny G track. By the time we got to the Florida state line I was feeling pretty good.

The drive was good because there was some traffic which made it interesting driving. There were plenty of 18 wheelers also. Sam closed his eyes and told me he would be ready to drive when I was tired or had to go to the bathroom, whichever came first. I knew which would come first because I drank all of my coke cola with dinner and took a to-go cup half full. It was nice that he did not judge me or condemn me for the joint. I had (3) more to last until I got to Jamaica. I was determined to chill. After another 2 hours I had to stop for a bathroom break. Sam drove the rest of the way stopping once before we got to Miami. We talked a lot about football, music, concerts we had gone to, cars we liked, politics and how we thought we fit in, my job, his career, what we use to do as children, and what we expect from a friendship. We talked about GOD and both wondered what the ultimate plan for our lives GOD had in mind. He loves the LORD and so do I so we could definitely agree with that. He did throw me off when he asked me not to be afraid of the gifts that GOD had given him. He said I would know him before we return to VA. The first thing that popped in my head was, 'Wonder if he is a warlock?

Is that how he knew me from a photo from 2 years before? What have I allowed myself to get into? Is this man too good to be true or real?' As if on cue he told me he was not a witch but had always been able to sense people and situations. He said he felt a connection or desire to know me when he saw me two years earlier. He said maybe he was just attracted to my fine body and smile. I understood that because now that we finally met, I knew I was very attracted to him. What I really wanted to know was if he could satisfy me sexually.

Men talk a lot about what they can and will do to you but most of the time they aren't equipped to back up their words.

Well, Sam was going to have to break me off one way or another during this cruise.

I was horny as all get out and was not taking 'No' or 'let's wait', for an answer.

If he didn't know before now, he would soon find out that he was gonna give me some and if he didn't bring it right, I was gonna rag on him til he cried uncle.

Now I was all into my thoughts not knowing if it was the high or would I really do it. No it wasn't the high. Coach was mine, at least on the cruise.

Then again, what if he was like Cee and his group? I laughed out loud thinking I couldn't be that lucky. He asked me what I was laughing about. I lied and said Frank and Sean would be so surprised if they knew he found the woman in the photo and it was me all along. He smiled and said, 'sure that's what you were laughing about.' I defended my answer then said, 'blame it on the joint!' He said okay we will see. He put his large hand on my thigh and squeezed. He reminded me that we had a suite with a king size bed and I would be sleeping with him, not one night but (7) nights.
He also reminded me that he hasn't been with a woman fully, ever and that he had not had sex with a woman in 10 years.
But he had plans for me. I told him ditto. Stop talking about it and be about it.
He laughed and said, 'remember your words, woman.' I responded also in laughter and said, 'you remember them.'
We had listened to music, talked and sang all night. Even though Sam was perceptive, he fell into the trap with his x-wife. He said he knew she was not in love with him but he was lonely and thought he could make it work if he gave her what she wanted, money.

He said he was in his 20's and had not matured enough to know that you can't force a relationship if both hearts aren't in it.

Sam was 48 and I was 52 years old. It was now 6 am and we had just passed the sign that said welcome to Miami-Dade. I had slept for about an hour or so but had a second wind.

Day One

Check-in was normally at noon but Sam made arrangements to check-in early. We would sleep until it was time to listen to the speech about the lifeboats. We arrived at the port and parked in the garage, unloaded the truck and walked over to the terminal. The ship was already there. The bag men took our bags. We went to VIP check in. They seemed to have all of our information already. Sam put money on my card and his. He paid the tips in advance. A man came out to speak with us. He and Sam exchanged smiles and hugs. Turns out this was, The Captain of the ship and Sam knew him. We went to our suite that had a balcony and was near the LIDO. We were not too far from the elevators so our walks would be short.

Good looking out. Sam said the porter had already cleaned our room to include the drawers but I sprayed them anyway with Lysol and sprayed the mattress with bed bug spray. He called the porter in from a nearby room and asked him to make the bed again because I sprayed it. The porter was glad to.

Sam informed him that we would like the sheets changed every day. The porter agreed.

He also told him not to go into our drawers or closets and to empty the trash every day. The porter agreed. I was impressed with the way he gave orders but made it sound like the idea was mutual. I sat on the couch and watched. I may have to use this someday. We both crashed across the bed. Too tired to speak! I couldn't say who fell asleep first. We didn't undress, just feel asleep. The road had whipped us good. Seventeen hours of driving was fun but hard. I was awoken by a kiss on my cheek. We had slept for four hours it was now noon. I felt a little refreshed and hungry. We got up, washed our faces, brushed our teeth and went to the LIDO to find food.

We didn't talk very much while we ate. He seemed to be studying me. I asked him to stop staring so hard. He smiled and said he couldn't help himself. He loved the way I look and wondered how I would look with red hi-lites in my hair. He reminded me that he was on a mission to win me. Finally, the formalities were out of the way. We finished unpacking, took showers and changed clothes. The ship was preparing to pull out so we went out on the balcony to watch.

The air in Miami was hot and sticky, but I moved close to Sam who lifted his arm to allow me access to rest my head on his chest. We were leaning on the balcony. He was just thick enough. I could feel his heart beating so he had to be human. We sat in the double chair still on the balcony and talked for a while. He told me he had invited a beautician to come along and do my hair. Her name is Sandy and she lives near the college.

She would be taking care of my hair daily and providing me with a massage when I wanted one. He made arrangements to get himself a massage daily, in a room near me. 'So is Sandy an old flame?' I asked. He said she was a hair stylist he met at a school function. He said he had already seen me so he wasn't interested in any other woman. Sandy knew this. Interesting! I wondered if Sandy really knew this. 'She is good people', he said. 'I promised to introduce her to one of my friends in Cozumel.' He thought they would be a match. I told him I don't normally allow friends I don't know, in my hair. He asked me to try and trust a little. The only products that will be used are the shampoo and conditioner his Godmother had sent to him, for me.

She said it will make my hair grow, the grey will turn to red hi-lites and my hair would be more manageable.

He said I would be meeting his Godparents when we ported in the Cayman's. That was days away, I decided to trust. We had already made plans to dip in the water of every port. My hair would have to be taken care of. The cruise was under way now. 'So Fro, how is it a fine woman like you don't have a man? I find it hard to believe there's no one interested.' 'I never said that, Sam', I responded. 'There's no one I am willing to trust with my heart. A booty call every once and awhile only because masturbation gets old and always experimental but my solution at the moment. A lot of men have an angle. They want to bang me without pleasuring me or want me to be a date for an event. They want me to cook for them. Am I getting close to your reason yet?' I asked. He smiled and said, 'not even close but I do like your cooking.' 'So I heard', was the only response I could muster up. Dinner was in a few hours. We decided to get out of the room and roam, to see who else was sailing with us. We both had on shorts and tee shirts. We started outside above the pool.

There were a lot of people and most were adults. The sail away song was playing. Everyone seemed to be drinking and letting their proverbial hair down. The pool was open and a few folks were in it but most were watching Florida fade into the horizon. It was on now, was all I could think about. As we passed the beautiful women and handsome men, they looked at us, especially Sam.

It's like they were trying to figure out if he was some celebrity. He was after all tall, handsome and built with little fat.

The sun was starting to set. The air was a little cooler but very nice. We walked further up the stairs to the front of the ship. It was windy but still nice. The glass or plastic in front was shaped like a windshield, there were chairs behind it. We sat down there.

There were a few others there also. I was curious why he hadn't found anyone else in the ten years he had been single. 'Sam, what's the deal with you? As fine as you are and all the groupies that follow the team, you mean to tell me there has been no one you were attracted to enough to commit to. All women aren't bad. There has to be someone you could have spent quality time with.' He said sure he has dated a few people and yes they were attractive and a few were downright gorgeous. He said they were not his equal in too many areas. They didn't really understand his commitment to football and coaching. They wanted the status and perks. But when the lights went down so were they. He said they couldn't manage their money or surroundings. How could he trust them with his financials if they couldn't handle their own? He said a lot of women want the man to pay all the time and they keep their change. This is true even with the professional women with careers. He said women have agendas too. Most women in my position for example, would be looking for a man who is stable and willing to contribute to their retirement fund. They want sex only on their terms and they wouldn't want to give up anything for the man.

Sometimes they play a pretty good game until you call them on it. Most women can't handle the truth, Fro! 'I'm the truth, Fro. I didn't know it at first but I know it now. I had a hard time when I tried to deny it but couldn't. I know who I know, what I know and how to use what I have been given. Baby, Can you handle the truth? Can you? Please say yes!' he said. I wasn't sure if he was asking a rhetorical question or not, but dude sounded like he was on something. I knew he had only smoked the cigar so I was a bit baffled. 'Sam, stop with the riddles. If you want me to answer you then ask me, straight, no chaser.' He smiled and looked around to see who was still standing or sitting around us. Everyone was gone. He turned toward the darkness at the front of the ship. He pulled me close to him and put my hand on his pants zipper. He motioned for me to unzip the zipper. I could feel a bulge inside. I unzipped.

He held my hand in place and pulled out his penis. He put one of my hands inside his hand and started laying his penis in my hand. He reached for my other hand and repeated the same movement. We were holding his penis in both hands. The ships light reflected a little. It was hard but not extremely hard. It was beautiful to me. He looked me directly in my eyes without a smile, but not a frown. He said, 'baby, meet my little friend.' I looked down at what I, no we, were holding. I could have screamed but held my composure. I squeezed lightly and said, 'hello my little friend. I've wanted to meet you.' I looked at Sam and smiled.

'Now this is what I'm talking about. Yes, baby I can handle the truth.' I reached over and kissed him softly on his lips. He removed one of his hands from beneath mine and caught my head and kissed me long and hard. Our tongues danced together. He sucked mine and then I sucked his.

His little friend grew harder in my hands. I rubbed him softly then squeezed. My hand could barely fit around him. I held him up and gently put him back in Sam's pants.

I moved in front of Sam very close and put my arms around his neck. I kissed him again only this time I kissed his lips and sucked on his lips, tongue and held his head in my hands. I closed my eyes and kissed him deeper than I can ever remember kissing anyone before.

I was telling him without words that I wanted him. He rubbed my back and held me close as I stood in front of him while he sat in the chair. When we could finally let go, I said, 'Let's skip dinner and see if I can really handle you and your little friend, please!' He smiled and said okay. I could feel his little friend softening. He moved me back and zipped his pants close. He grabbed my hand and got up from the chair. Without words we walked back to the room and put the 'Do Not Disturb' sign on the door. With this being the first time we would be making love, I told him I'd be right back.

I went in the bathroom and closed the door. I had to get myself together; this was a huge deal to me. It was his show so I had to pull up and allow him to take the lead. Woman you can do this is all I could say to myself. I washed my hands, rinsed my mouth with water, threw some on my face and walked out.

He was already lying in bed with the covers pulled back. He had a very seductive look on his face. I breathed deep and walked over to the bed. I pulled my tee shirt over my head and pulled my shorts off. I would let him do the rest. He said, 'come over here baby.' I fell into his arms. He kissed me on my forehead, then my neck as he did, he unhooked my bra. He kissed my lips, my mouth opened, he put his tongue inside and rolled me over at the same time. I was now beneath him. He lifted himself up, pulled my bra off and threw it on the floor. He moved down, kissed my neck and moved to my breast. He sucked the left breast until I moaned then moved to the right breast. He sucked it with such passion my vagina started burning then I felt him pull my panties off. He kissed and licked my stomach and pulled himself back up to allow his little friend to brush against my leg. I squirmed, pretending to try and get away. He repositioned himself. I moaned again and said, 'baby let me feel him inside me.

Let me see what he can do. Does he want her? Does he?' He said, 'you want to see, huh? I'll show you in a few. You have to let me have you, all of you, for a few minutes, if not an hour.

You gotta be ready for my little friend', he put his finger between my legs.

He moaned with pleasure. I was already wet, real wet. He said, 'my lord, baby'.

I smiled through my moan of pleasure. He must have thought I was being over confident when I told him I could handle his little friend. This vision was a sight for sore eyes. I have never been completely there. My husband was the only man who had come close but I had never been there... I always felt if I could run into that extraordinary guy with a dick to match, I would be completely satisfied in my personal life and could do the work GOD put me here to do. My total basic needs would be met. Sam doesn't know that I have always produced lots of juice, very easily. This style of love and sex is right up my alley. Just then, it hit me. What if Sam is the man I have always wanted and I'm the woman he's always wanted? I let out a heavy moan and allowed him to have all of me. Sam moved his penis to the entry of my vagina (my soft spot). He pushed his little friend and the head popped in. He rocked forward a few times giving himself a vagina head job. I pulled him more inside me. He moaned. I swirled my hips round and round about 6 times.

Three times slow, then three times fast. He said, 'oh baby' several times. It felt so good I just leaned with it, pulling him in deeper. I felt him throbbing, it was an awesome feeling. He moaned, 'baby, you okay?' I could only mumble 'um huh', while pulling him in even more. My body got warm inside. I was filling up with him. He said, 'baby I'm going all the way, you ready?' All I could say was 'umm'. The base of his penis touched the entrance to my vagina. He pulled back slowly and went forward again. I moaned with pleasure and so did he. We both rocked back and forth five times slow and five times fast. This was repeated 10 times without stopping. Then he repositioned himself straddling the entrance to my soft spot. He rocked back and forth fast and then slow. I let out a low yell. He said, 'where is it? Where is the spot?' I was so dazed in pleasure I could only say, 'umm'. He repositioned to the other side and started the same count. Five fast then five slow, this time when he went in, he touched something that made me jump. He did it again, slower this time, when he got to the spot where I jumped, he stopped. I screamed in pleasure. 'That's it! Ok.'

He pushed in and out pausing on the spot. I could only rock in pleasure swirling my hips in rhythm with his pushing in and out.

He put the tip of his little friend on the spot and rubbed it hard and fast. I had an orgasm over and over until I begged him to stop. He said, 'No, I want you baby, say yes!' Just then it felt like I passed out but awake at the same time.

(A still, soft voice said 'He is him, Fro! From me to you, I do love you'.) I heard myself saying 'Thank You' over and over. Then I was awake again, feeling Sam throbbing inside me. He said, 'I'm not letting you go woman.' His strokes got harder and faster. I was already exploding with an orgasm. He said, 'I'm here, I got you baby'. I felt his orgasm spray on the same spot. I screamed in pleasure, holding on tight to his back. He slowed down and moved his little friend away from the spot. I was so relieved. I tried to control my breathing and slow it down. Almost there!

What the hell was that, I was asking myself? Sam was still semi hard and repositioned himself to face me. I closed my eyes so he couldn't see me. He was still half way inside me moving very slow.

It was like a cool rub down after a massage. What the hell have we done? We just made love or close to it.

A voice other than mine, spoke to me and said Sam was him. I couldn't remember what else it said. Sam used his fingers to open my eyes. I grinned. He had a priceless, satisfied look on his face. I tried to look away and he kissed my cheek, then my neck. I turned the other way with the same result. I stopped in front of his face. He kissed my lips and opened my mouth with his tongue. He found my tongue. He wrote 'told you'! I pushed his tongue out of my mouth. I didn't want to admit he was right because I didn't know why he was right.

I didn't want him to be full of himself or play games with me. He held my arms down so I couldn't move. I pretended to try to get away but the slow movement of his little friend inside her felt so good. Finally, sex and love with a wind down instead of a full stop. He said, 'baby that was unbelievable. It feels so good to be with a woman I like, have something in common with and whom I can freely make love to without feeling like I'm hurting her and running into the possibility of a rape charge. Baby, I can't let you go. I need you so bad.

You know you need me too, I know you want me woman.' I was thinking, Ok Fro, be a big girl and stop torturing this man. Give him a chance to prove he's true. Ok I will give him that. He caught me off guard, because he went hard up front. But I let him. I'm gonna hang back and see if this is just fun or if he is serious. Wonder why I heard that voice? Sam repositioned himself and laid beside me to hold me. I moved closer to him also. I didn't want to miss a minute of this... whatever it is.

There were a few things I wanted to know also. 'So did I pass the test? My bad, this test?' I asked. 'You know, you passed. Now what?' he asked.' He said he was hungry, it was 8 pm and we had not eaten since lunch. Dinner started over an hour ago. He said, 'Let's go anyway, late.' He wanted me to dress after all of that work and no shower, not happening. I told him I needed 30-45 minutes. He called the dining room from the phone next to the bed. He asked that dinner be held for us until we get there in an hour. 'Anything else?' he asked. I said, 'okay, you go first in the bathroom.' I went through the closet to see what I was gonna wear. I had a red, hi/low sun dress with tan 2 inch sandals and red amber earrings and bracelet.

That should brighten a late dinner and my sore back wouldn't be noticed. I ran in right after Sam came out of the bathroom and let the water run especially over 'her' and my back. We were ready for dinner within 30 minutes. Our server was ready as soon as we sat down. We looked at the menu and ordered everything at once.

He kept smiling at me like he had a secret. He said he just noticed I wasn't wearing makeup.

I wondered if that was bad or good for me, but didn't ask. We ate with minimum conversation. We tabled dessert. After dinner, we went to club deck to take photos. We looked around the clubs and saw a few groups dancing but chose to pass and get some rest since we would be porting in Jamaica tomorrow. We went back to our room and went to bed. Sam started rubbing my behind. Thinking this was a request, I turned over so he could get some from behind. He did. It was very good too.

Day Two

It was tomorrow already. We would be coming up on Jamaica in two hours. I was up first, then Sam. He said we would be leaving at 8 am. His boi, Michael would be waiting for us. He had plans for me and a little business meeting for him, today. He asked me to shadow him. I asked him to explain.
He began to tell me about Jacob, his childhood friend. He takes care of Jacob financially because Jacob is physically handicap and his parents are dead. He visits at least twice a year. I asked how Jacob was handicapped. Not realizing that question would change my reality as I know it now.
He said this man loved this woman to death. Literally! He was jealous with his girlfriend. She finally told him they could no longer date. He got so outraged, he raped the woman and during the act, he got sperm from a male alligator and inserted it into the woman's vagina. He then had sex with her also. The lady got pregnant right away. She had the baby. A boy! He was normal looking at first then grew a tail.

He couldn't go to school so Sam brought school stuff home and helped Jacob study. Some people were afraid of Jacob but not Sam. Jacob's mom had a Dr. from a nearby village cut the tail off so Jacob could have a normal life. Jacob almost died. But the tail started growing back and Jacob began to heal. Sam knew the tail would never be able to be removed but Jacob still had life and wanted to live. Sam made it his mission to help care for Jacob even as an adult. I thought that was the most selfless act I had heard in a long time. I almost shed a tear but I didn't want to fall for a trick.

I have several handicapped relatives with deformities. It would not be a shock nor would I prejudge anyone.

He went on to say, he and Jacob, have something else in common. 'Jacob will explain'. Now I'm wondering what's up.

He said he wanted me to stand behind him when we went into Jacob's room. He said don't be scared because Jacob will know. Trust! Jacob can't hurt me because he would be hurting him. And he won't do that. Their relationship is too deep.

He said he trust me with his life information that no one else knows, besides his closest people all of whom live in the western island chain. He said no one at the college knows what I'm about to discover. Now me being curious had to hear him say it. 'Sam, why are you sharing this information and why have you chosen me to share this with? You don't really know me.' I said. He said, 'Yes, I do!'
I asked if Jacob was wild or something. Would he attack me? He laughed and said it's nothing like that. I told him to tell me why I should be shielded by him.
He said Jacob can read my mind but not when I'm behind him. I told him that GOD covers me and I'm not afraid of a man. He said okay but if I get scared, grab his hand. Jacob will feel the connection. By the way, he is blind. All I could say was, 'Alrighty then!'
We were talking and moving at the same time. I wore a bathing suit with a cover shirt and sandals. Sam wore trunks that looked like shorts and a button down sports shirt. We made our way to the deck where you exit the ship.

I asked Sam about Michael. He said he was physically intact but he loved to run women. He knew he would have a good time with any woman who ventured off the ship and in his path. I laughed.

It was 8:30 am when we walked out to the street to look for Michael. I looked over to the right and there was this pretty silver jeep. A guy with long dreads was waving his arms. I grabbed Sam's arm and pointed. He grinned wide and yelled at Michael. His language changed. I could barely understand him now. He was speaking Patwa. We walked over to Michael. Sam grabbed his hand and hugged him hard. He pulled me to him and said, 'this is she, Fro'. Michael pulled me to him and hugged me tight. He said, 'you finally found yo man huh? I responded that he found me. He laughed and said, 'I see, Miss Fro not sure yet. I know my boi gonna do it'. I responded, huh? He laughed again. Bro, you should have taught her a few words in Patwa. Sam told him he had a hard enough time getting me to agree to come he couldn't add anything else. They laughed.

Michael said, 'so Sammy, you got de woman runnin from you for a change'.
Sam looked at me and said, 'I don't want her to run away from me, I want her to run to me'. I ignored him while getting into the back seat. Michael was looking at me up and down. He smiled and looked at Sam. Sam shook his head, smiled and got into the front passenger seat. Michael was about 6ft or a little less. He had a lot of muscles and was dark but not black. He had braids not dreads. I asked him why. He said he likes his hair to be loose sometimes. He had someone who would braid it whenever he wanted it. His hair was curly but not straight. He had beautiful teeth. I asked how he stayed so fit, he said he swam almost every day and played soccer in his spare time. He said he has been busy lately because Sam has been working him hard. Sam responded, work good for you, boi. More work, more money. Michael agreed.
He said, 'Sam, you want to go to da house first? That would give Jacob a chance to wake up.' Sam said yes but he was calling Jacob now. He asked Michael for his phone.

He greeted Jacob and told him to get his lazy ass up. We would be over in an hour or two. He hung up without waiting for a response. The ride wasn't long to get to Michael's house or so I thought. We turned into a gate entrance off the road. Once through the gate there were (2) houses, one up on a hill and the other to the right of us. The one on the hill was some type of stone. It looked like it was medium sized. The one to the right was stucco. It was larger with two floors. Michael told Sam that the house was prepared. He drove pass the stucco house and made his way up the hill to the stone house. He stopped half way. Sam told him to call when it was time to go. He said, 'man you can drive yoself. I will see you later. I got stuff to do; you know I don't rise this early.' Sam shook his head and agreed. We got out of the jeep and began to walk the now short distance to the house.

He knew I was thinking, where are we going and who's house is this. He said that this house was his house. The land belonged to his mom but was his when his mom died.

He said he wasn't there enough to need a bigger house, so he let Michael build his house on the land so he could keep an eye on Sam's house. It made sense. We walked in the front door. I was pleasantly surprised. The floors were wood with a few rugs. The furniture was nice with rust and yellow tones. Most of the furniture was made out of some type of wood. He said wood lasted longer in the salt air of Jamaica. Metals would rust faster. The front area was open and airy. Curtains, not blinds draped the windows. The place was cozy. He showed me the kitchen and poured some juice for both of us since we had not had breakfast yet. The stove and the air conditioner were gas which had the house nice and cool compared to outside. He said he was fortunate to be close to a natural gas line. His expense for the up keep of the house was low. We went to the first bedroom. It was large with a window on two sides. There were two twin beds next to each other with a table between them. The beds were up high from the floor, and made up military style. He said you don't want to make it easy for bugs.

There was a large flat screen TV with a Wii game near it. There was also a love seat in front of both windows. The room had a ceiling fan also. We moved to a smaller room that had office equipment in it. There were plaques on the walls but I didn't go to them. We walked pass a bathroom with modern fixtures and tile. Then we got to the back of the house and his bedroom. It took up the entire back of the house. King sized bed with one level of pillows. A TV attached to the opposite wall. There was a nice sofa near the window. There was a walk in closet with a suit and shoes and a few shirts hanging up. Boxes were on several shelves. The bathroom was on the opposite side of the room. It was large with a separate shower and tub. The toilet was in the corner with a partition separating it from the rest of the bathroom. There was a double sink and a window next to the shower. Sam went back into the bedroom and sat on the couch near the window. He held out his hand for me to join him. I came over and sat right in his lap.

He held me close and kissed the back of my neck before turning me sideways. He started a kiss that lasted longer than expected.

He said we did get up early. He asked if I wanted to take a nap. I smiled knowing he didn't want a plain nap. He wanted a nap with benefits. I was more than willing to engage. I had not had this kind of sex ever and I was determined to enjoy every ounce of it just in case. He carried me to the bed and pulled back the covers. He undressed me first which didn't take much and then allowed me to watch him undress. He had a fairly hairy chest with a few curly hair locs visible. I was turned on just watching him undress. He pulled his pants off very slow. His little friend was rising with every move. I was smiling and getting wetter by the second. His little friend was hanging half way down his thigh. I was amazed I could handle that much meat but glad for the opportunity. I'm sure Sam was happy. He leaned toward me as I opened my thighs.

He pulled my nipple with his teeth very gently. The pressure was electric which made me moan in pleasure. He kissed my stomach and moved down to my soft wet spot.

He looked up at me looking at him. He said it smelled good and he wanted a little taste. I protested because it was so wet. He said please, just a taste he wouldn't go far for long. Even though, I was not ready for that intense of a feeling, I shook my head, yes. I bit my lip as he stuck his tongue in the wet spot and licked once, twice and all of a sudden he was massaging the wet spot with his lips. The feel of his lips moving in and out and knowing they were wet with my juice, made me squirm. He looked up at me and licked his lips slowly. She was beginning to beg for more of something, anything to reproduce what she had just felt. He blew into the wet spot slowly. I almost jumped out of bed. He caught my legs and held them steady. He came back up and let me taste his lips while he allowed his little friend to get close to her. I grabbed his little friend and guided him to her entrance. Sam pulled my thighs apart further and pushed all the way in. I swallowed hard and let out a small scream. He didn't ask if I was hurt this time. He knew I was adjusting well to him. He positioned himself like he was going to do pushups.

He rocked back and forth and pushed in as far as he could go. He looked up to the ceiling and moaned with pleasure. He pulled out and repeated the same movement again. I wrapped my legs around him when he went all the way in again. I didn't want him to come out before I came which wasn't gonna take long now. He positioned on his elbows and pushed in and out similar to last night but slower. I was feeling this man and he was making sure I didn't forget the spot. He found it and rubbed it hard with his little friend.

I came fast and hard. I held on to his back and swirled my hips around and back and forth like I was scratching a pole. I couldn't control the noise that was coming out of me. I stopped trying to hold it in. 'Baby, that's it! Right there! Oh Baby yes.' I didn't want to say it but was compelled. He put his hands underneath my behind and raised me up to meet him. He pushed in and out and round and round for what seemed like an hour before he said, 'this is for you baby, he pulled back until I screamed from him touching my spot.

Then he pushed in and moved my hips to his rhythm while he sprayed my spot. I felt like I was melting into him. I rubbed my face into his chest to ease the overwhelming helpless feeling I had, at that moment. He was really having his way with me and I was happy to have a helpless feeling while allowing him to give it to me how he wanted to. Ten years had to have created a backup. It would have for me. We laid there with legs wrapped up, panting like animals. It was kind of funny but I couldn't laugh. Sam had never made love in this house before this moment.

I was proud to be the one that finally brought love to him in his house. He said woman you are wearing me out. I said ditto. We both laughed because we knew that was far from the truth. We had to pace ourselves or we would be too sore, or so I thought.

I told him I should be able to lose the 10 lbs I wanted to lose by the end of this cruise. He said I was fine the way I was and if I had questions about losing my belly fat, his Godmother could help.

We fell asleep in each other's arms for almost 2 hours. The phone rang.

It was the house phone. Sam answered and said sorry we fell asleep. He laughed and said I'm not lying we did.

Okay was how he ended the call. That was Jacob. He's been waiting for us. Let's take a shower together and head out. It was noon when we left. Sam drove a black jeep that was in the garage. He said Michael keeps it up for him.

He talked while we drove to wherever we were going. He said, 'the business is called, 'M & S Exports'. I asked what business is that. He said him and Michael owned a business. That's what the initials stood for. He said they export jewelry and have a few contracts mainly with the cruise lines. They provide jewelry for the ships to sell.

I asked how the business is doing. He replied it was doing well. They have made a profit every year for the past 5 years. He said he splits his profits 5 ways. (Jacob's care, his house/car, savings at offshore banks and an athletic fund at local upper schools)

He also puts money back in the company for overhead. No wonder he has money for a cruise I thought.

I was excited to see the company and more excited to be riding in a jeep, in Jamaica with Sam driving and knowing where he's going... he seems to be happy here.

Guess his heart is here because his mom is buried here, he was born here and lived here to higher school.

Fro, what have you gotten yourself into? You are not trying to get married again no matter if he is Coach Maxwell. But Lord knows this man has put it on me.

The building was set in the middle of a major road with a neighborhood on one side. There were escape plans to move Jacob if needed and fast. That was so detailed, sounded like plans I would have made for the same reason. We pulled up and Sam parked in the closest park with someone else's name on it. I'm thinking they know you here Sam, ease up. I would have walked my ass right in from across the parking lot so they see who he's with. That is being a show off.

I want to be on vacation with a handsome man who is trying to date me but knows his money can't buy me so he is blowing all my other senses.

Introducing me to his family and screwing me in his house, the first time he's ever done that. We are making history moments here. We were walking into the front reception area. There is a gate here and someone has to let you in. Great idea helps to stop robberies. Sam clicked his key fob and the gate opened all the way through. That got Michaels attention. He came over and grabbed Sam's arm.

I interrupted and asked could I look around and buy something? Michael said, 'I'm sorry, Fro.' Let me show you around a moment so you know what you're looking for'. Sam told Michael, he could do that. Michael told Sam he got this. Michael showed me a few things but I was interested in butter amber. He said it and Jade are in the same category.

I told him I would be okay while they talked. While looking through 2 bins of different amber some with shapes and some without. A piece caught my eye. It was gorgeous. It had a created shape. But I didn't know of what. There were earrings to match so a ring and earrings are good. I can afford this myself. They were still talking so I looked further over and saw the diamonds. They had different colors. Colors I liked. There was a cardboard tray with all sides up about 2 inches. I picked yellow, red, chocolate, light yellow and light chocolate or caramel colored diamonds. There was a piece of paper on a table. I got it and started making my shape with the stones, I chose. It was like a paisley drop. The yellow would be the accent stone.

The red would channel around the yellow, the chocolate would help the light colors. It would be set in white gold or platinum.

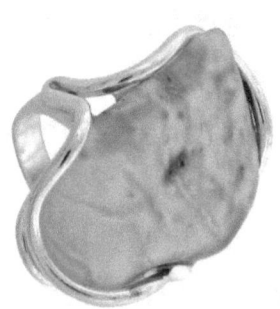 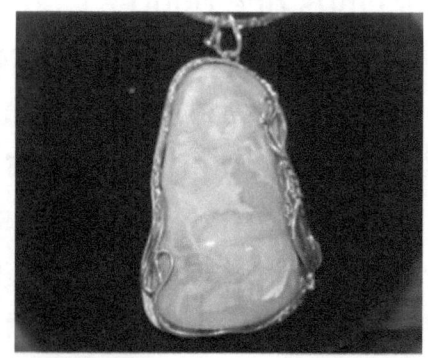

Sam walked over, I showed it to him. He liked it also. He told me I had good taste. I said I know.

I asked him to ask how much it would cost if it's real and how much if its 10k gold overlay. He said okay and took the tray. It will be put together like you asked and they show you a photo before you decide to buy. I agreed. He went in a side room. I showed the butter amber to Michael, he laughed out loud. I asked why. He said Jacob was working on this piece using the same amber. That's his signature symbol and he made the pieces himself. Get the hell outta here. I told Sam it's time to meet Jacob.

Sam said, 'Do you remember what I told you?' I said yes. Initially Sam's words were taken to my heart but when I saw Jacob in a seat in the back of the room I felt drawn to him. Wondered if this is what Sam meant. He greeted us but stopped and held his head down. Fro, you are more beautiful in person. Come here woman and give me a hug. Sam said, 'J. what did I tell you man, don't scare Fro.' I wasn't feeling this over protective thing. What was he gonna do bite me? I bite back so that won't work out for him. He smiled and Sam laughed.

What was the joke between these two, I wondered. Boyhood memories creeping up from the past.

Jacob asked me again for a hug. I was tired of the hiding thing. I pulled Sam's arm and held my hands up. Sam smiled. I walked up to Jacob and leaned towards him. I hugged him without closing my eyes. The tail was there. It was moving side to side. It was about 4 or 5 feet long. It was brown in color and it didn't look wet.

My heart softened and I kissed him on the cheek. 'Hi Baby, It's nice to meet you. Sam told me he's known you most of his life. You two love each other huh?'

Jacob said, 'Yeah, he my boi'. Michael said he would be back.

'So I see we have similar taste in butter amber. I love the pieces you made. I'm buying the ring and earrings. They are going to put gold lever backs on the earrings and the ring fits perfect. How did you know my size?' He said he asked Sam. I don't remember telling Sam because I don't remember him asking.

I can see old friends playing tricks on new friends. I didn't take kindly to being tricked. I went for the juggler.

'So Jacob what is it that Sam won't discuss about you or himself?' Jacob told me that he is a Seer. He can tell what you're thinking without you saying it. I asked what the difference between seer and clairvoyance was. He said not much accept he knows his comes from GOD. He can hear you from miles away. He knows when folks have good intentions or bad. He said Sam can do the same thing.

I turned to look at Sam. No he didn't set me up. He looked at me with a look that said, I knew you wouldn't believe me if I had told you myself. So you have been hearing me all this time. I was kind of pissed. But could I have not thought anything or could I have controlled my thoughts? Probably not!

Well now he knows I like him. But he also knows I'm not easy. Integrity matters more than anything he can do materially. He better hope GOD has reserved some of my thoughts from him. His feelings may be hurt. I hope he heard that. He looked at me and held out his hand. I took it. Jacob shook his head.

He said, 'Fro, you got him. He's not gonna let you go, he's waited too long for you woman.' Sam squeezed my hand. I changed the subject. 'So Jacob what is the symbol on the amber?' He said it meant 'Eternal Love' and it was not an accident that I found it.

He left it there for me to pick. He said he knew I would. This is his signature line. He's gonna be presenting his line when a few pieces get recognized. I asked him how this was getting done. He said, 'you are gonna present it for me, Fro'.

He told me he was making a necklace and he would have it ready before we left to go back to the ship. 'Jacob can I come see you again sometime?' He said, 'I will see you sooner than you know. If you Sam's woman you are a friend of mine.' I said thanks Jacob and I hugged him again. He held me longer this time. Since he was blind I allowed him to feel me. Sam found my hand again and signaled for me to come on. I told Jacob I will see him later. He said ok, cool.

When we went back up front, I stopped Sam and looked him in his face and said, 'Really?' He told me he didn't know how to tell me.

He apologized if the revelation hurt me. He said he didn't mean to. I said okay. What else could I say or do about it. Nothing! Michael called me over to him. He had the lever backs on the earrings and the ring was in a box. I asked him how much, he said Jacob paid for them. I yelled, 'Thanks Jacob'.

He hit the floor real hard in response.

Michael said Jacob has something to give me before I leave for the ship.

We paused when I saw the ring I created on a monitor. I was speechless. I turned and Sam was right behind me. He said it was real nice. I said yes, I want it, but I don't want to be greedy. He said if he gave me the ring I would have to wear it on a regular basis. I thought, Oh, like an engagement ring? Sam smiled and said, 'I wish'. I shook my head, yes. He said someone would bring it when it was ready. We were going to a day party at one of his favorite spots. There would be people there that knew him and people he knew that he had not seen lately.

Michael arranged for food and drinks. I am on vacation and this is Jamaica.

I did want to try some good native food, and hang out where Sam use to. Maybe we can vibe.

We left the shop with Michael driving.

He asked me if I wanted to hit his smoke. I said yes. He smiled. He puff, puff passed. I laughed thinking of my work colleagues. I puff, puff, puff passed. Now Michael laughed. He passed it to Sam who puff, puff, puff, puff passed. Michael pulled over on the side of the road, got out of the jeep and laughed. It made us all laugh. But what were we laughing for? Sam was high! Well, well.

I wondered about him. Another thing no one else knows. He winked at me. I smiled. I asked Michael for a few already rolled for the cruise. He gave me (10) joints. I refused the blunts.

We got to the beach party about 2:30 pm. The ship would be boarding at 5:30 pm. We pulled up to what looked like a large outdoor gazebo. Screened in! I smelled something good to eat right away.

I got out and followed Michael and Sam. They spoke to a few folks and went inside.

The people there seemed friendly and happy to see Sam.

They looked at me and whispered. I know they wondered who I was to Sam. Well no sooner than we got there Sam stopped the music and said hello to the people and thanked them for coming. He introduced me by my name, Fro.

He told them he was trying his hardest to convince me to date him but I wasn't sure he was on the up and up. He told them GOD sent me to him and he had feelings for me. He told them she like yo boi, a little more now. I hit his arm.

He was teasing me and I was not falling for it. The whole time he spoke it was in Patwa.

I could understand most of what he was saying but filled in the blanks for the rest.

There are a group of females sitting together. One of them is kind of giving me a dirty look. I wanted to meet her. Maybe she was an old neighbor who had some juicy information or maybe she was an old flame. Either way, we will speak, I was sure of it.

Sam told them that they would be getting a raise in pay.

I tried pretending I didn't hear him say it but the positive smiles and claps made it obvious. I looked at Michael. He smiled hard and shook his head. I clapped too, feeling out of place. So these are employees of the business. No wonder I didn't see very many people when we went into the shop. This was the business meeting.

I touched Sam's arm and pointed to the food. He smiled and said I was eager to try Jamaican food that was real, not American. They laughed. I found the plates and started in. Only picking what looked good. I wanted plantains more than anything else. When my plate had no more room, I looked into the crowd of people already seated, so I could sit and eat. There was a table in front of Sam, it was empty. I made a bee line for a seat there. Sam was still talking but I was not listening now.

I had the munchies bad and had to stick one of those plantains in my mouth right away. They tasted just like I liked them but better. I closed my eyes as I chewed. When I opened my eyes, Sam was looking at me smiling.

He said, 'Baby is that good? You look like you having a good time in yo own world'.

I smiled and thought of the recent sexual encounter with Sam and thought I liked that more than plantains but so far not by much.

He said, 'Okay, you can't talk?' I said, 'Mr. Sam this taste so good, why you messing with me? Have you run out of things to say at this meeting?' He laughed, playing it off. He said, 'touché'.

Michael put his head down and laughed to himself. He said out loud, without yelling but loud enough for me to hear him, 'Sam, boi that yo woman yo raisen'. I almost responded to Michael but Sam looked at me and said No, with his look.

I started eating my food again. Sam said, 'Fro not agree to be my woman yet, boi.' Don't scare her. Michael laughed and responded that I was not afraid of them, I was afraid of him. The ladies at the nearby table laughed out loud. I reached over and held my hand for a high five.

One of the women gave it to me. Everybody started laughing then.

Sam looked at me and said okay he would work on that. We laughed again. Sam yielded the floor to Michael who talked so fast in Patwa I could only make out a few words.

I glanced at the woman who had given me the evil eye. She was agreeing with Michael but looking at Sam. Sam looked at me, looking at her. I was thinking, so this is who likes him here. Wonder has he felt her up before? If she were able to handle his little friend, he may have kept her because she was pretty in her own way.

I finished my food and got up to put my plate in the trash. They had Jamaican beer and Dos Equis. It was warm and I was thirsty. I grabbed a beer and found the opener nearby. This time I saw an opening next to the woman who was watching Sam. I didn't even look at him.

I sat right next to her. She seemed startled. I ignored her response. Michael saw what was happening and called me out. He asked me if I wanted to say anything. He said these people were their friends and most worked at the shop. The woman looked at me like, 'now what?'

I thought I should clear a few things up now just in case Sam and I become partners. 'Yes, I would!' I said.

I moved away from the table and turned to the people sitting. I thanked them for not making me feel totally out of place and for making me feel welcome.

I told them I would treat them the same when they visit me. I didn't know about their business until I got to the island. The woman looked at the other woman next to her. I told them I was blessed to meet Sam's people. 'Sam is a very special man to me and I'm trying to decide if he is for real or making an attempt to use me for something I don't want to be used for, and it doesn't matter to me, what he has, like this company.' I said. 'I am feeling yo boi though. Lord knows he's fine as hell!'

They all laughed and Sam put his head down. Michael interrupted and said, 'okay, you having too much fun. That's enough.' Sam ended the meeting which turned out to be their yearly meeting.

He signaled for me to come over to him. I did.

He said he had to go out and talk with Michael for a few minutes and asked if I would be okay. He said not to be mean to the woman. She worked at their office and he knew she liked him but he was not interested in her that way. He said she may come off defensive because of her feelings. I promised to be on my best behavior and not rock the boat any harder than it had been already since he brought me there without telling me the details.

I would have dressed differently. He said, 'no baby, that's not what I mean. You dressing in a swim suit is fine.' Being upset that other women liked him would be crazy as hell, under the circumstances I thought. He said, 'yes, that'. I agreed. The women were still sitting, eating and talking. I went back over where they were while Sam went outside with Michael. I sat facing the women but didn't speak. They were already talking in Patwa, really fast. They stopped after their conversation had wind down. The woman who gave me the evil eye asked me had I met Jacob. I told her I had. She said you agree Sam should keep him like that.

I said I was proud of Sam for protecting Jacob all these years and I was impressed with their sense of family and how they protected and loved each other.

She seemed to soften, a little. One of the other women asked me if I was in love with Sam. I said I wasn't sure, but I really liked him. I told them how I had not been looking at men much after my husband had passed. But Sam found me and was trying to convince me to date him because he thinks we are meant to be.

I asked the woman who liked Sam, what her name was. She said, 'Monee'. I said, 'So does Sam already have a woman here?' She looked surprised at the question but the other women smiled and looked at her. She said, why do you ask? I said, 'I don't want to come between anything already in place. That will give me a reason to tell Sam, we can't date!' She asked me not to tell Sam that, he would be unhappy. So I'm thinking she can't have that much in common with Sam if she doesn't already know he is a Seer. She said she used to want Sam for herself but he never asked her to his house.

I asked what did asking her to his house mean. Another woman said it means the man wants to see if you feel right with him in his space. This is how they know you fit and they can keep you because you can be trusted in their house. I thought that sounded logical.

Now, since Sam had made love to me in his house, in Jamaica, what did that say about me? Did he trust me? Did I fit?

I already knew the answer and so did the ladies. Monee asked me if I had gone to Sam's house. I told her no, not in the USA but I had gone to the house here in Jamaica. She shook her head, knowing we could have gone to Michael's house but we went to Sam's house. She said, 'Did you and Sam?' I said yes.

Monee put her head down and a single tear hit the table. One of the ladies fussed at her in Patwa. She said Monee know she not Sam equal. She knows Sam got a large manhood and she can't handle that.

She said Monee just want Sam cause he from Jamaica and she knew him as a boy and always liked him. He was always nice to her too. She said Sam a man now, Monee. He knows who he like and looks like it's gonna be Fro.

He never brought a woman here before, not even that woman he married long ago. Monee agreed.

She looked at me with a smile this time.

She told me that she was angry with me at first because she always wanted it to be her that Sam wanted to be with but now she has to be happy for him. He found me and I am good people. I asked her how she could tell. She said I was bold and stood up to Sam and he still wanted me. She said Sam called and told them I was coming and Jacob was very excited. He started making his symbol out of that yellow stone. She said he must really care for you. I blushed thinking the same thing. But why?

The other lady said it didn't hurt that I could handle Sam sexually. No one else has been able to say that. I thought it had to be more than sex. I would have agreed to be his sex buddy without the extras.

Sam and Michael returned and a reggae song was playing. Sam came over and grabbed my hand to dance with him. I did.

We danced for two songs when Michael's phone rang.

He told Sam he would be right back. Sam said we were gonna take a dip in the water over at the beach. We turned to the door. I turned around and the ladies were watching us. I waved at them. They waved back. It was pretty warm by now.

It was almost 4pm I knew we had to leave soon, so I caught a few waves knowing my hair would be an afro, afterwards. We played in the water. He held me close to him and rubbed his little friend between my legs. I tried to run but he held on tight.

He said one day we're gonna make love right here in this water. I thought how that must feel great. He smiled and kissed me deeply knowing the people in the gazebo were watching but he didn't care. No sooner than we got out of the water, Michael pulled up. He had a medium bag with the 'Eternal Love' symbol on the bag. I said, 'for me?' with a big grin on my face. He handed me a towel first, then the bag. There were 4 boxes inside. One box had Sam's name on it and the other (3) had my name on them. Michael promised Jacob he would take a picture of my reaction. I wondered why since he was blind.

I opened the long box. It had an amber necklace, bracelet and ankle bracelet inside. They were very lovely. I hugged them while Michael took the photo. I opened the bigger box. I had to sit down... There was a dress inside. It was almost the same color as the amber and very soft.

It was a halter dress with high/low concept. I even brought shoes that would go well with it. I smiled with tears in my eyes hugging the dress to my chest. Sam smiled too. Michael said, 'Damn boi, when he had time to make that?'

I yelled very loud, thank you, Jacob! I love you too. All of a sudden I heard a yell that sounded like the hootie hoo call. Sam and Michael laughed.

They knew Jacob could hear me. I yelled again, 'Jacob you hear me?' He yelled hootie hoo back. I opened the last box. The ring was stunning. All the different color diamonds and the paisley pattern worked.

When I picked it up, I knew it was platinum because it was heavier than white gold. My heart almost stopped. I showed it to Sam. He took the box from me.

He said, 'perfect.' He took the ring out of the
box. I said, 'Sam is it...' he stopped me before
I could get it out. 'Yes" was his answer.
I was going to ask him if it were real. Wow!
It had to cost a lot. Sam said, 'yes', again! He
motioned for my left hand. He said, 'Baby,
this is a token of my feelings for you. Think
of me when you wear it.'

I smiled and tears fell from my eyes. He wiped them away. Michael said, 'awh' from behind the camera.

Sam pulled me close and kissed me with so much passion I got weak. Michael said, 'ease up boi, she leaving with you'. I laughed, so did Sam. I thought this must be a dream, how did this man happen to me. I am really feeling him. But what does he really want from me. I tabled the thought.

It was getting to be time to go back to the ship. We said goodbye to the people in the gazebo who seemed tickled at the site of my afro. Monee looked at my hand. She smiled at me and said, 'Sam is your man, Fro. He picked you first but you will pick him too. Enjoy'.

Sam told Michael he wanted to drive his jeep back to the house and Michael could take us back to the ship. It was 4:30 pm. Sam and I got back in the jeep without going into the shop. It didn't take long to get to his house. He pulled into the garage and sat there for a moment. He told me his mom would be proud of him and happy that he was happy with me. He said whenever I come back to Jamaica I would be staying in this house.

I told him I would be happy to. He asked if I can show him once more. I knew he was talking about sex. We went into the house and put all our things beside the door. We walked naked back to his bedroom and this time he laid on the bed first. His little friend was at attention. I crawled over him and got on top. I rode him soft and slow! He held me tight and turned me over. I was on the bottom now. He went straight for the spot. I had an instant orgasm he pushed and pulled a few times before he came also. He left his little friend inside while we both caught our breath. This was the cool down that I was beginning to get use to. He pulled out and we jumped in the shower together. Within 15 minutes we were back in our clothes at the door. We walked down to Michael's house. It was a short walk and the view was beautiful. I looked back at his house thinking I will be back. Michael dropped us at the gate for boarding the ship at 5:25 pm.

What a nice day I thought. Sam smiled. Once back on the ship we put our bags away and Sam called to see when would be a good time for my hair and his massage.

They told him it would be at 6 pm so we went out on the balcony and smoked. He had a cigar and I had one of Michael's joints. Sam took a hit of the joint. I could only think that this man is finally free to act normal with a woman. I was glad the woman was me. He told me he was glad it was me too. He said he wanted to see me in Jacob's dress and asked if I would wear it tonight for dinner, I said yes. I got up to go look for the shoes and lay the dress out. It was perfect.

We finally left to go to the spa deck for treatments. Sam introduced me to Sandy. She was a pretty, Spanish looking woman. She had to be about 30 years old.

Her hair was cut really cute and her smile reminded you that she must have been a cute baby.

I wondered how Sam could pass on her. Wonder what he knows about her that she doesn't know he knows. This was gonna be a trip, I could see that already. I was gonna have to hold some cards to my chest. I wasn't telling her anything she didn't already know. But I was curious how she could keep a fine man like Sam close but don't touch.

I would not have been able to resist trying with him. Even if he said, 'no, let's be friends. I already saw my soul mate I just have to wait for her to come to me.' I would have tried until she came. So wonder what her side is. I know Sam knows but won't tell me. I can guess he wants me to develop my own relationship with Sandy.

Smart move on his part! Sandy seemed shy around Sam but when he left the room she could breathe again.

I wondered why she did that. She asked me how I wanted to wear my hair. She didn't see me before my afro appeared. I told her we would be taking photos every night and I would be wearing different outfits. I told her about the halter dress for tonight. She said she would think about it and tell me before, to see if I like the idea. I agreed.

She told me about the shampoo and conditioner from Sam. She said it smelled very good. She started washing my hair, which felt great, the salt water was beginning to make my scalp itch.

She rinsed and washed a 2nd time. This time she said, 'wow, your hair feels silky'.

It was tingling a little. She washed the soap
out and commented how rich it looked.
She put a handful of the conditioner on it.
It felt great and soothing on my scalp. My
scalp felt like fingers were massaging it.
Sandy looked at my hair and said, 'oh my'. I
asked her what's wrong. She said my gray
streaks just turned red. I asked if she meant
neon or subtle. She said subtle but it changed
before her eyes caught it change gradually. I
said ok. She said that my hair had lain down
and grew about 2 inches. She showed it to me
in the mirror. I like it but not sure of what
was happening. I asked her to rinse the
conditioner out now. She did but I was left
with a head full of beautiful hair with red
streaks where the gray was. We both smiled.
She blowed it dry and it was still silky and
curly to wavy. A strange combination. We
both liked it and decided to leave it like that
just so Sam could see what he had done since
the shampoo and conditioner were from him. I
didn't tell her it came from Sam's Godmother.
I wore my hair parted down the middle and
hanging. It looked like a perm.

By this time Sam was leaving his massage and was waiting for me. He noted it was nice, he liked it. I was thinking to myself what has he done to me. What's gonna happen when the shampoo and conditioner are gone? Will my hair fall out? I can't see him doing that to me. He smiled at me. Sandy and I didn't talk much because of the shock with my hair. When we left the spa floor, I had to ask him what gives. He said he didn't tell Sandy where he got it from because that wasn't her business. He hired her to take care of my hair not divulge his family secrets to her. This answered my question from earlier. He had not told Sandy everything about him. This let me know where she stood with him. Now what about her! We dressed for dinner. The dress was hot! Sam could hardly take his eyes off me. The jewelry set it off.

It wasn't large and gaudy. It was small and sexy. And butter amber stone does what it does. It fades into you, like it's wearing you. The paisley ring fit right in. Sam said, 'my woman, Lordy, Lordy'. I walked up to him, put my arms around his neck, tip toed up to his lips. I kissed him on the lips.

He reached down and kissed my lips and sucked my tongue and wrote, 'I want you' on my tongue. I swallowed and sucked his tongue in response. We ate dinner slower this time and made small talk with the maitre'd. People noticed us right away. Some people stared like they were trying to figure out who we were. We saw a group of sorority sisters and fraternity brothers across the room from us. I'm thinking that's great, one of them was bound to know Sam Maxwell. Sam turned his total attention to me. He made note that my hair was cute and he liked the red hi-lites. He loved the smell too. He made me get up to look at the dress. He commented on how the bra was so true to size. He wondered how Jacob could do that.

I made another comment about me wanting to lose my stomach. He reminded me, Nan would help me with that. He said with or without my belly, the dress was nice and looked beautiful on me. I said thanks. He reached across the table and kissed me. It was so romantic. We left dinner early because we were still full from the Jamaican food. We took photos. I posed sexy with my leg across Sam's thigh.

We posed in a kiss. And then let the photographer pose us how he thought we should look with our outfits. Sam was just sexy for no reason.

We left there and headed to the club. The DJ played (2) songs for us to dance to once we got in and found bar stools. They were slow dances. We had a good time dancing with each other. He is a very good dancer. He put his hands on my hips and rubbed, I started getting hot and wet too.

I squirmed on him like he was really my man and we were about to make love. Could he be right? Is he my man? He smiled. We went back to our room and undressed for bed. Tomorrow we would be in the Cayman's. I was more excited by this stop than Jamaica. I loved the Caymans but it was hot. Sam said we would rest at Nan and Poppy's. Poppy would be picking us up at the port. We locked the jewelry up before we went to bed. I kept the paisley ring on. I told Sam I was not here to sex him every night but he couldn't keep his hands off me, who was I to stop him? I was getting great pleasure in the process.

Day Three

The next morning came early. But we got up
and started dressing. Sam asked me to wear a
sundress or shorts because the sun would beat
me less. I agreed.
We left the ship to catch the transport boat
to shore. The water was just as I
remembered it, really blue. Almost didn't look
real.
We were walking across the street when Sam
spotted Poppy. He was standing outside his
car. He looked to be about 70 years old. He
saw Sam and perked up. They hugged tight. I
smiled. He pulled me to him and said Fro, this
is my Poppy. I love this guy. Poppy said, 'Oh,
Sammy, you know you my boi.' He said hello
and hugged me too. It felt genuine which
made it feel good. He was shorter than Sam
and a little heavier. He had grey hair and
mustache. He was handsome for his age. I
was imagining Nan.
Poppy drove a Mercedes that was dark gray.
He said lets go, she waitin for us.
Sam rode in the front. I looked out of the
window in back.

I knew I wanted to go to the Tortuga Factory before we left. Sam turned around and smiled. I'm thinking what's up with him. More surprises? I couldn't have imagined. The drive took about 15 minutes. I saw the sign that said Tortuga 3 miles ahead. I was happy that we were not that far away.

We turned into another gated property. It was nice and bright, in pale green, pastel colored stucco. There were two floors. We drove around back. There was a pool right off the back patio. It looked so inviting. We would have to take a dip. We got out of the car and a grey haired, light skinned lady appeared. She was smiling from ear to ear. She grabbed Sam and pulled him close to hug him tight.

She said I missed you baby. He kissed her forehead, both cheeks and her hands. She blushed. She spoke to him in what sounded like a form of Spanish and Patwa, mix. He responded the same way. They laughed and she turned to me. She told me to come on and love on Nan too. Sam introduced me as, Fro! He said her name was Nanette. I smiled and hugged her like she was my auntie.

She squeezed me and kissed my cheek. She turned toward the door and said 'come on in now'. I followed her but Sam went toward Poppy at the trunk of the car. Poppy wanted him to help get something out of the trunk. A smell pierced the air, it was plantains. They were fresh on the counter. I asked could I take one. She said eat my child. I cooked for you and Sammy. He said you like jerk chicken breast, white/rice and plantains. I shook my head as I swallowed the delicious plantain. She stirred something on the stove then said Fro, baby Sam told me you want to lose your stomach fat and tone without losing much weight. I shook my head as I took the last bite. She walked towards the bathroom and motioned for me to come with her. I followed. She went into the bathroom which was very large. There was a chair in front of the shower that she told me to put my clothes on. She said she wanted to see what I really needed but needed to see my body first. I hurried out of my clothes and left my panties on. She felt the weight of my breast and felt my stomach. She turned me around to look at my back and my behind.

She went into the bottom of the cabinet where the sink is and pulled out a large jar. She looked at my hair and said, 'I like the color the shampoo made your hair turn. It fits you.' 'So will my hair come out once I don't have any more of this shampoo? Should I expect my hair to go back to the way it was?' I asked. 'Oh, no baby. Nan knows her ingredients. This is your hair from now on. Without the shampoo and conditioner it would grow a lot slower but I'm sorry, it won't go back.' I wondered how Nan knew all of these things. I thanked her for helping me. She told me it was her pleasure to love on, help and befriend Sammy's woman. She told me I was her girl now too. I almost cried. She continued with what she was about to do. She opened the jar and dipped her fingers in it and pulled out a big heaping of a blue cream. It reminded me of the water surrounding the island. She rubbed it in her hands and began to massage it on my breast first, then my stomach. She put some more on her hands and put it on my back where my bra normally rest. It felt cool all over like mint was on my skin but it was not hurting.

I asked her what that was. She said it was 'tortoise cream.' She said it absorbed the excess fat and firmed your skin. All of a sudden I felt my breast start moving. They were drawing up tighter. It startled me because I thought my breasts were shrinking. That's what it looked like. They stopped when the nipples were pointing straight out. Before I could get excited I felt my belly start drawing in. I said 'wow', my breast looked nice in the mirror. My fat belly seemed to melt away but it was actually drawing in. The skin tightened and I have to say it felt funny. The fat on the side of my stomach melted and the skin drew up until it was smooth. I actually have muscles in my stomach. It was so nice to see them after so many years of hiding. I could feel the effects on the top of my back. Looking in the mirror now I noticed my behind was large, so were my thighs. Nan asked if I wanted to just tone my bottom, I said yes but I didn't want my hips and thighs to disappear. It took too long to grow them. She laughed. She put the top on the jar and took out another jar that read mild. It was lighter blue.

I told her I could do it but she said no, she needed to do it to show me how. I pulled my panties down, then off. She rubbed the cream on my behind, thighs and my upper arms. She asked me how was the sex with Sam? I blushed and said, 'How do you know if there is sex with Sam?' Nan said she has never seen him so calm. It seemed like he was satisfied or on his way. I laughed out loud. She said, 'what? I know a little about these things.' All of a sudden, my hips started feeling tight, so did my thighs. They still seemed a little thick but less giggly. My arms tightened also. All of this in less than 15 minutes.

She said, 'now get in the shower and use your hands to rinse all the blue stuff off.' I followed her instructions. She sat in a chair and waited for me. She came over and wiped the blue stuff off my back. I got out of the shower just in time. I had to pee really bad. She pointed to the toilet just like she knew I would need it. When the pee came out, it was blue but it kept coming then it turned regular looking. When it stopped I asked did I pee out all the fat. She said yes. I told her the sex with Sam was great.

I have never been with a man like Sam. She
said I never will again. I asked what she
meant by that. She put the cream back and
pulled out a bottle of what looked like lotion.
She asked if she could apply it since she
probably never would again. I agreed. I
waited for her response about Sam. Nan
seemed to be a wise woman. You could hear
her confidence when she spoke.
She told me that Sam has been waiting for me
for years. He knew I was out there but didn't
know how to find me. Nan said the day he saw
me at the college, he couldn't contain himself.
He called her crying. He said that I was real
and he knew it when he touched me. He asked
her for advice because he didn't want to run
me away. She said she told him to first thank
GOD for his mercy and grace, then start slow
to become friends. Then introduce me to his
family. Taking me on a cruise would guarantee
I could not run from the truth but adjust to
it. GOD would do the rest. He finally calmed
down. She said only a few women in this world
can be with a man like Sam. I was one of that
few and Sam was not about to allow me to
leave him.

Not in a mean way but a loving way of possession. She told me he needed me, my love, passion and hands on. Nan said now that she's met me, she knows he was right.

She pulled out a small bottle of oil, it was dark in color. When she took the top off, I smelled a faint scent. It wasn't stink but musky like with a sweet after smell. She said I would need this sometimes. If I put a dab at the opening of my vagina, it will help keep my vagina in healthy shape.

It will help with its elasticity. Nan said you have a man with a large penis that over time will stretch you out. This conch oil will keep you good and it will attract Sam to you more. Be careful because it will attract others also. Only use when you feel discomfort during love making. Try it out now. I put a dab at the entrance of my vagina and put my underwear back on. I asked Nan how she knew all this stuff. She said that's a conversation for another day.

She said she will ship me a few bottles of oil, lotion and the blue cream. She will give me a bottle of each now.

I thanked her for helping me get rid of my extra fat. She said, 'I see you like plantains.' I said, 'yes'. She said that was good because they good for you. I told her I wanted a Cayman smoke. She said of course. I have some under here and she looked under the same cabinet. She pulled out a zip lock bag full. I held my head down and smiled. She said, 'what? Nan need to relax sometimes too.' I said okay and laughed. She laughed too. Once my sundress was back on we walked out of the bathroom. Nan went to the kitchen for a smaller baggie. She put (10) joints in the baggie and told me to put all my things in my bag. She took out another joint and handed it to me. She went back in the bathroom to store her stash and returned with a bottle of each cream she rubbed on me. I put everything in the bag I brought with me. The house was open and airy. The furniture was nice but seemed expensive.

You could see a balcony upstairs and what seemed like bedrooms. She saw me looking and told me Sam can give me a tour. She said lets go out to smoke. I followed her to the back by the pool.

We smoked a few puffs, it was smooth. She said this was her good stuff. The high is mellow.

Sam and Poppy came over from the garage. They were catching up. Apparently Sam had not visited in a while. Poppy said, 'woman let me hit that.' Nan passed it to him and he passed to Sam who passed it back to me. I was good after that. She was right but it was kinda hot outside. She told Sam they had to go to work for a few hours. She said food was on stove and a room was ready upstairs when we wanted to rest. She smiled at me.

She said, 'I left a few things for you, Fro.' I asked why. She said because she wanted to. I thought okay.

She told Sam to bring me by the factory, a little later for a tour.

I asked where they worked? She asked, 'didn't Sam tell you?' I shook my head, no. She said, 'Tortuga Rum.' I felt faint. 'No way', I said. 'Yes way', she said. I looked at Sam. He smiled. Nan said she and Poppy were the owners. I could have passed out.

I screamed, 'rum cream'. She said, 'We know, Sam told us. We got you.'

I hugged her and kissed her face. I did the same to Poppy. He held on a little too long. Nan said, 'told you'. I knew she was talking about the oil. So did Sam. He heard our entire conversation. Nan and Poppy got in the car and pulled away.

I turned to the water and asked if we can get in. He said yeah. I took off the sundress and Sam grabbed me around my waist. He turned me and looked at my body. He said, 'damn.' What am I gonna do with you, Fro?' I responded, 'the same as before.'

He reached down and kissed me, searching for my tongue but I wouldn't give it.

He pulled off his shirt and shorts and made his way to the deep end of the pool. I took off my panties and entered the pool on the shallow end. The water felt wonderful. I went under a few times while Sam watched me. He called me to come to him. I knew I wasn't a great swimmer but managed to make it to him anyway. With a very sexy grin on his face he held me up while he treaded water. He was a great swimmer he told me. He moved us back to the 6ft area. He could stand up here.

He ran his hands down my body and shook his head. He told me I clean up nice. He reminded me he told me Nan could help me. I told him Thanks and kissed his lips. The sun was beating us now. We got out the pool, grabbed our clothes and went in the house. He brought out (2) towels.

We draped the towels around us, sat at the kitchen counter and ate. The food was so good I couldn't believe it. Sam said he has always loved Nan's cooking.

She cooked for him and spoiled him for years. He learnt about business from them.

He grabbed my hand and led me upstairs for the tour. The house was beautiful. He took me to the room that Nan made up for us. Sam said it use to be his room.

He pulled the covers back and led me to his bed. He sat and pulled me to him. He said that scent is intoxicating. His little friend started growing. It was hard as a stick and pulsating with anticipation. He picked me up and laid me on the pillow. He didn't talk. He kissed me so passionately I almost lost my breath. I was really feeling him now.

He went straight for my breast, sucking one, then the other until I moaned with pleasure. He was really enjoying this. He kissed my belly and made his way to my soft spot. He licked a few times and softly kissed her. We both were feeling something magical or so we thought.

He came back up without continuing that way, put his little friend at the soft spot and started pushing and pulling as he went deeper. We got into a rhythm quicker than before. We were kissing and stroking at the same time. All of a sudden I felt like I was dozing off. It felt like I was asleep but awake at the same time. Everything was quiet.

I recognized the still soft voice from before. This time I knew Sam was there also. I could see and hear him, but not with my ears. It was like a dream.

The voice said, 'Do you believe me now? I can't lie! Sam is your man from me. He is as special as you are to me. Don't be afraid.'
I wondered was I dreaming.
The voice said, 'No, you are not dreaming. I am allowing both of you this time to learn to love each other. You woman are the newest to be in my presence this way.
He believed me first for a chance to be with you.
You need him as he needs you. I need you both. My work has to go forth. I am allowing you both 40 years of rebirth to do my work. No sickness will be fall you.'

HE said, 'Woman your recent past will be thrown into the sea of forgetfulness with regard to the sexual encounter with Cee. It has already been erased from him. I have never and will never allow Sam this knowledge.'

HE said, 'Sam, she feels afraid you will forsake her and deny her when it suits you. She's afraid of being rejected by you once she allows you to have her heart fully. You have to convince her.' HE said, 'You both have been provided with tools you need. I love you both.'

I felt myself awaking but Sam was zoned and going for his. He had my legs up in the air above my head gliding from side to side. It felt very good. He rubbed my hips and squeezed my thighs. I rubbed his head and pulled at his short hair. He pulled right to my spot and stopped. 'Baby, I love you. I didn't know for sure until The Father spoke. This is for you.' He put it on me so strong, I screamed with pleasure and said, 'I love you too, baby.'

Unlike before, I remembered what I heard this time. GOD spoke to me. Sam said, 'yes, HE did. We have 40 years of good health. But we have to do what HE wants us to. We will be rewarded during this time and in the end as we know it.' All the time Sam was talking he was slowly moving back and forth, cooling us down, sexually. This had been the best so far.

I wondered what Sam wanted from me nevertheless. He had to have a plan and I wanted to know what it was. We laid in his old bed and made love again without intercourse. He kissed and caressed me until I was filled with total satisfaction.

I was making this man work, or was it me that was working? I have allowed him to have control during this cruise. He looked directly at me and responded, 'I have not been in control, GOD has.' I couldn't argue with him on that one. We laid there for awhile longer then got up to shower. I noticed some yellow clothing on the chair. He said Nan gave them to me. It was a bathing suit with cover and sandals to match. It was beautiful. When we got out of the shower, I put it on. It fit very well. Sam said, 'you are so sexy baby with that on.' I had to agree. He had new trunks also. We went downstairs and ate more of the great food Nan had cooked.

She called and asked Sam to give me the two bags on her bed.

She meant to give them to me before she left for work. There were two extra swim suits with matching shoes.

Using Nan's car, we made our way to the Tortuga Factory up the street. Sam pulled in the first available parking, as usual. We went in to an awaiting Nan and Poppy. They were happy to give me a personal tour. It was so fascinating.

They had mini bottles of rum cream. I took a lot of them. Nan said she would send some when she sent the other items. Everything will be shipped to Miami. Poppy told me that he has been putting money in Sam's account for the past ten years. He said he was proud to be able to match Sam's father's contribution. Sam asked him how much. He said 10 million. Sam looked at me and shook his head.

They just want grandbabies around here, was his comment.

'Fro and I can't have any babies, Poppy.

But she does have grandbabies that would love to come and live here. He said that was nice but he wanted our baby to come stay. This time I shook my head and smiled. I could see Sam getting a surrogate to take my egg and his sperm and carry a child that we would allow Nan and Poppy to keep. We had other agenda's for now. That thought was so far off. We said goodbye to Nan and Poppy before we caught a cab back to the port to re-board the ship. Sam didn't want to inconvenience Poppy by having him drive back 15 minutes.

We road in silence for a few miles before we started talking about our experience. We didn't need to speak out loud. Sam had the cab stop at the bank before we got to the port. He said he wanted to check his funds. I was going to stay in the cab but Sam told the driver to wait and watch my bags as he insisted I go in with him.

He was greeted by a beautiful woman who addressed him as Mr. Maxwell. He smiled at her and asked if she could help with an account. She walked back to her office, we followed her. Sam had four accounts. He asked the lady to add my name to two of his accounts. I looked at him in surprise wondering why. He didn't answer me, he just asked for my ID. I was slow to give it. Still wondering why he was doing this. He added me to his personal account and the one Poppy and his father had deposited ten million each. She asked him was I his wife. He answered, 'not yet'. I was stunned. She gave me a card with the account numbers and balances. I was blown away. Sam, a millionaire! I would have never thought of him as such. He was so down to earth.

He said his father and Poppy had the account number and deposit money in this account. Sometimes he doesn't know how much is there. He said he hasn't used it in years.

She gave me her card with email and such on it. I asked her to withdraw a thousand dollars in US cash for me. She did right away. Sam laughed and said, 'What, you didn't believe me?' I put the money in my bag as we left the bank. The cab was still waiting. I didn't say a word out loud but was laughing to myself. I asked him, please tell me why? He said, 'You are worth more to me than money, haven't you figured that out yet?' It was my turn to say, 'touché '. I said to him without words, I will not betray your trust.

We boarded the ship and made our way back to the room. I took the pretty swim suit off so I could wear it tomorrow. I laid the others on the bed. We looked at them admiring the fact that Nan didn't know what my actual size was in advance but got them and they fit. It was nice to have my stomach reduced without pain or being cut. I even really liked my breast.

They were the same size but tightened so they don't look so heavy. All other imperfections I wanted to keep. This was overwhelming to me. Who is Sam? What does he really want with me? I knew I was special in GOD's eyes and a few others. I saw so many other women that seemed like a better fit for Sam then me. I wasn't gonna let him be my dictator. I don't care how much wealth he has or shall I say we have. I can't believe this dude. Putting my name on his bank accounts in the Caymans, What a move!

Sam asked me to come sit by the bed with him. There was a sofa there. We sat on the sofa. He had already heard what I said. He held my hand inside his and massaged it gently. He kissed my forehead then my neck. He smiled without teeth and began to speak out loud.

He said he knew I was a little overwhelmed and he understood because if the shoe were on the other foot he would question my motives also. But he wanted me to allow him to prove himself, that's all he's asking. He has been totally amazed seeing my interaction with his family.

He said, 'They love you and want you to come back. That alone says a lot, Fro.' He had a point but I normally get along with most people, naturally. Baby, I am not trying to be yo boss. We got a boss and that's GOD! Did you hear what he said? I believe him don't you? Point again. 'Only thing is I have never experienced this. I know you have a reason for sharing all of this. Sex might play a part but it's not the biggest part.', I said. Sam looked at me and laughed out loud. He said there is no way he would let me fade from his life. The road trip is too much fun right now. He said he has always dreamed of being with me.

I have to admit I am having fun with Sam on this vacation. So far it's been twist and turns and I know it's not over.

This is only the third day. Sam was looking a little tired, I have to admit the Cayman sun and heat kicked my tail. I was a little tired myself. The intense sexcapade wore me out. My stomach growled. Sam smiled and said, 'My baby is hungry huh?' I couldn't help but lay my head against his chest and hold on to him. He held me tight too.

After what seemed like an hour, we put on our robes for treatments. Sam's massage, my hair and maybe a massage for me too was a welcome thought.

Sandy was waiting for us with all smiles. She asked how our day went. I gave her a mini bottle of rum cream. She said this was for later. Sam went on to his room and I stayed with Sandy. She washed my hair three times because of the pool water. She commented that my hair was behaving nicely.

She conditioned it and it grew another two inches. I was pleasantly surprised.

Sandy wanted to put my hair in a style. I let her. I had a black dress that I wanted to wear. She put my hair up in a cute style. I liked it. She finished ahead of schedule so I asked for a massage. She agreed. It sure felt good. This was my chance to see who she was. 'So Sandy how long have you been in this business? She said she was 31 years old and had been doing this for 6 years. She said she didn't have any children and no serious boyfriend. I asked why not on both accounts. She laughed and said which came first, the chicken or the egg. I laughed too.

She said she wasn't ready to be called mom yet. Also she had not met anyone that she would want to have a baby with. She was trying to build up her business. I certainly understood that. I had to ask how she knew and met Sam.

She said she was at a college concert and happened to be seated next to Sam. They talked about the songs.

She saw him again at the barber shop next to her shop. She was interested in him but he already had his mind on me. There was no chance for a relationship. She said she knows when to back off. Sam asked her to come and he would introduce her to his boi. She said his name is Carlo, and she was getting excited to meet him. I asked if she was still interested in Sam. She said no but she wanted to remain friends. She asked me if that was alright with me. I told her I had not made up my mind yet, if Sam and I would date when we returned to VA. She asked why not. I told her it is all happening so fast. Something seemed off and I couldn't call it. She said Sam was a good man and he was deserving of a good woman.

He believed that to be me. She said he needs his own woman in his corner.

I told her that I really was feeling him but wasn't 100% sure. She asked who was or would be 100% sure of anything.

I told her if I found out Sam was playing me I would not date him, no matter what. She laughed and said, 'Fro, you don't know what you're in, do you?' She said, 'that man has been looking for you, for two years. He seems happy every day I have seen him on this ship. Something is going on. You done blew that man's mind haven't you?' I smiled and said, 'not intentionally but he has really blown mine.' I have a hard time accepting the fact that I can satisfy a man like Sam. Just then he came out of his room and into mine. I knew he heard the entire conversation.

We went back to the room and went on the balcony for a smoke. He was smoking a cigar. By now I was mellowing out. Sam and I had been together for almost 4 days to include the ride to Miami.

I wasn't so overwhelmed in his presence anymore. We got dressed for dinner. We ate slow, laughed, talked and kissed during dinner.

He liked the up hair and the black dress. We had fun taking pictures too. We decided to go to a few clubs on the club deck. Sam wore black also. We caught men and women's stares. When we walked into the club that we attended before, the DJ saw Sam and played music Sam asked him to play. But tonight the soro's and frat bro's are in the house. There were about 20 females and 30 males. They were laughing and having a good time. It was nice being in their presence. I had to go to the bathroom. I left Sam there. When I returned, two females were talking to Sam. One was sitting in my seat. They were nice looking women. I heard one of them say, you are fine as hell. The other said we can turn you out boo!

I cleared my throat and responded with, 'the only woman in here that's gonna turn this one out is me.' They turned around like they got caught with their hand in the cookies. One of them told me not to leave him alone too long someone might snatch him up. I moved in front of Sam, put my arms around his neck and kissed him passionately. He kissed me back and rubbed down my hips.

They both said okay and walked off. When I came up for air he smiled at me and asked why I was signifying. I told him I was protecting him. I laughed this time. We danced a few more songs and left. We walked up on the deck. It was very nice. People were looking at a movie outside. I didn't want to look at any TV while we were vacationing.

We walked some of the food off from dinner before going back to the room. Sam wanted to smoke so I smoked also. We went to bed after another hour or so.

The night was eventful in that his little friend slept outside of my soft spot all night. He did not enter at all. We sleep nude.

DAY FOUR

Day 4 was here and there were no ports today. We finally got up and dressed.

I wore the yellow swim wear that Nan gave me. I looked cute in it. Sam wore a t-shirt and his school colored trunks. That man had to know how fine he was. He made my mouth water. I couldn't be mad that the ladies pursued him. Under general circumstances I would look too even if I didn't pursue. He grabbed me by my waste and said do you really think I'm sexy? I kissed him long and felt his butt. I finally answered yes.

We went to the LIDO for food. Lots of people were there. I saw some of the soro's in the day light. They were still having a good time. Sam went around another side for some other food item. A brother that looked about 30ish came up behind me. He said, 'hello Lady'. I smiled and said hi.

He told me I was beautiful in that swim wear. I said thanks. I got it in the Caymans. He asked if I were with someone, I said yes. 'You married?' he asked. I said, no. 'You engaged?' I said no again.

He said, 'will you dance with me at the party tonight in the piano room. I told him, yes, if I go. He said cool and walked off. I found Sam and we found a table to sit and eat. Afterwards we went out on the open deck to people watch and maybe get in the water. There were not many chairs left vacant. We finally found two. The Caribbean heat was nice but required a dip in the water every once and awhile. Sam wanted a dip now. I wasn't ready yet. He went in. I was near the water. He splashed me. I took off my cover and jumped in. He pulled me under right away. He held my nose. I finally calmed down and came up.

I asked if that was how he was taught to swim. He said Poppy did do that to him a few times. I smiled thinking about how cool that old man had to be, to be with Nan. She was something else but I could see myself growing to love them both. Sam heard me. He said, 'I know right?' I smiled wondering if he heard that guy ask me to dance tonight. He splashed water in my face and said, 'yes'. I bounced up to his face and said, 'you aren't jealous are you?' He said, 'you are!'

He reminded me how I acted last night. I laughed and said, 'you're right'. I got out of the water. When I went to sit back down, I noticed the same guy who spoke to me earlier was watching me and smiling like I was new meat. Sam got out and noticed also. He was smiling too. He told me the guy was wondering if he could hit me up on this cruise. Sam said, 'over my dead body.' I smiled hard. I said, 'and you know you got 40 years so you can't die no time soon.'

I laughed. He turned around like he was gonna get back in the pool.

He scooped up some pool water and ran over before I could run. He threw it on me. I yelled! He started tickling me and wanted me to take it back. I kept saying no, he kept tickling and started feeling my thighs and tickling them. I finally had to say okay. I take it back! He caught my face and kissed me. He stuck his tongue far in my mouth. I swallowed hard and he eased up and finally kissed my lips before he sat down. I was dizzy. I pretended to fall out into his chair on him. He said I better behave or he would be forced to do something to make me scream.

Oh boy he is right. He can make me scream for sure. Okay, I said, 'truce.' He said wise choice. I thought wow look at this, he wants me to think he has serious feelings for me. He picked up my hand and kissed it. He said he was sure he was in love with me.

He said I was his baby and he would protect me as he should. I almost cried. I believed him at that moment.

I was having a hard time owning up to my feelings but I think I love him too. I don't want to though. Am I ready for that? Even if I'm not, he is making me see that I should because he will and can satisfy me. I know I can satisfy him, in more ways than he knows. I suppose it wouldn't hurt to let my guard down a little. How did you find me love? I was hiding from you.

He said finally some head way. You hard woman! 'No, I'm not,' I said. He said, 'yes you are. You try to play innocent but I believe I know you are capable of great things. That's why I will have a great time watching. You know you know how to win friends and influence people.' 'What you think you know about me Sam?' I asked.

'You'd be surprised, Fro', he said. I'm ready to go back to the room. I thought I need to smoke. He said, 'me too.' We started gathering our clothes.

We had to pass the soro's and frat's on the other side to get to our room.

As we got close to them, I saw the lady from last night. She yelled, Coach! Everybody looked at her than at Sam. Aren't you a UVA Coach? I bet you are. She was smiling. Sam smiled and shook his head. He said he was, so what! She said, 'can you come to our party tonight? We would love to talk with you and dance and stuff.' We were still walking. I stopped. I thought to myself, I know this chick didn't just disrespect me for No reason. She don't know me or Sam. Sam said, 'baby, ignore her'. I said, No! I turned around and walked over to them. I paused a few feet away. I said, 'my name is Fro, if you want to know all you have to do is ask me. Sam and I are on vacation and I'm glad we are on this ship with you all but I haven't done anything to you for you to disrespect me.

You were talking to me when you asked Sam to come to your party. He won't come to your party if I don't agree.

She said, 'Coach, I thought you were single with no girlfriend. That's what you say in your bio. I looked online.' 'Is that right', I said. I got closer to the woman. I said, 'do you believe everything from the internet?' Without turning around to look at him I told the woman, 'Ask him who he said he loves. Ask him? She looked at me hard. Everyone close was watching and I'm sure recording by now. Ask him? I repeated. The guy behind her said, 'Hey Coach, you love her? I mean, Fro? I turned around and looked at Sam. He heard me say, baby this is your opportunity to come clean and tell me. I'll believe you if you tell me right now. Sam smiled and looked over at the woman and then the man. He saw all the folks stopped and waiting for his response.

He said, 'yeah man, I love this woman. More than even she knows.' He looked at me. I smiled at him. I turned to the woman and said, 'so as I said if I don't agree, he won't be at your party. So are you inviting me also? Cause Sam is not coming without me.

We are dating and no one else is ever going to have Sam again. I love him and I don't share. I turned and he was close to me now.

He pulled my arm and put it around his back. He reached down and kissed me very softly. The woman said, 'okay, Fro, do you want to come?' I said, 'we'll think about it.' We walked off and moved towards our room. Sam was smooth. When we got to the room, we found the smoke and went out on the balcony. We both smoked in silence. I left to go take a shower, Sam followed me. He washed my back. I washed his when we traded spots. We fell in bed after the showers. We needed a nap. But Sam had to know for himself.

He said, 'Fro we're dating okay?' I said okay. He said I won't regret giving him a chance. I told him it will take some time to let my guard down it's been up a long time.

He said ok but don't make him wait so long. We kissed passionately for awhile. Before I knew it, I was asleep. Sam went soon after me.

It was time for hair and massages when we woke up. The sleep was needed though. We left to go to the spa deck.

Sam greeted Sandy. She seemed bubbly.
'Have you two been online this afternoon?' We
both nodded, no. She had her iPad and turned
it around to us. There we were on You Tube!
Sam shook his head. I smiled and said, 'I got
played huh?' Sam said he didn't care if they
posted that. He kind of knew they would. He
held my face and reminded me that there are
no backsies. I couldn't take it back anyway.
Sandy washed and conditioned my hair.
It still grew. She gave me another cute style.
I wore a tan shirt dress w/ a belt. Sam wore
a silk suit with sports shirt. The silk looked so
good against his skin. We left for dinner.
Sam made an announcement to our close table
mates. He made me blush. He said, 'she
agreed to date me. Meet my new beautiful
lady ya'll!' They clapped. Sam was so happy.
I was glad he chose me.
My mind couldn't stop thinking about the fact
that I know Sam has something he wants from
me but won't tell me. I wonder which one of
us will get our blessing first.
We decided to go to the party for a little
while to rub elbows with the soro's and frats
on the ship.

Show them how we work it, while getting tips from them. I didn't want to harbor ill will toward the ladies that liked, no loved Sam. He was the truth and so was I. They couldn't handle our truth.

So they would have to admire from a far. Sam was now off the market since the video. Sandy had shared that the video got so many hits. It went viral fast. Sam was a major college football coach, people paid attention to him. The women knew Sam had not been dating, but didn't know why. There was once a rumor that Sam was gay. Too bad people judge without facts. Wow, Sam was free. I freed him. He can now date, have sex and have a real relationship with me.

I didn't know how to be anybody else. I would have to pretend and there are days when I don't want to. Could that be why he was given me? Sam said, 'Fro, snap out of it woman. You freed me, okay! Let's talk about that later. They are waiting for us.' 'Behave, Fro.' 'You behave, Sam.'

When we finished our pictures, we went down the hall to the club. I was gonna have to get use to being watched.

With the stomach gone and breast lifted I
was wearing the hell out of most of my
clothes. Sam has noticed.

Can't wait til we make love again to see what
it's like. Tonight will be the first time since
dating has started. We went into the club.
They all noticed us. We found an empty table
and sat. The ladies came over. They asked if
they could take Sam. I said yes as long as you
bring him back. Sam, said, 'baby you good? I
said yes. No sooner than Sam left did the
frat brother appear. He asked if he could sit
for a minute. I hit the seat.

He said his name was Charles. He is an
executive at his company. He is single and 30
years old. He wanted me to know if things
don't work out with Sam, please, please give
him a call. He said he knows why Sam needs
and wants me. I said really! Why? He said my
ora, is powerful and I don't realize it. You are
probably the only woman in here with no
makeup on and are beautiful anyway. He asked
if I can cook, clean my house, pay my bills and
have some degree of financial stability.

I said yes to all of the above. He said this
shows in my body language and my words.

He said I have an ability to meet people on their level and that showed earlier today. He said with you on the team it runs better. Coach Sam knows exactly what and who he has.

He said he ain't mad at the brother just appreciate him sharing at this juncture. He said he is looking for a woman like me. He also needs a true partner so he can move on to other things he wants to do in his life but have his woman to hang out with. I told him thanks for saying that about me but I don't see that as different. That's normal to me. He said, 'that's my point! You still know this. So many women don't.' 'GOD's gonna bring somebody honey.

Don't be weary in waiting. Let's dance.' I danced with him for 3 songs. Sam was waiting for me when we left the dance floor. Charles told Sam he was fortunate, take care of her. Sam dapped him and said, 'I plan to do exactly that.' I told him to stop hating. I know he heard me even though I didn't say it out loud. Sam and I danced for 2 songs. They were love songs and made me want to screw him right on the dance floor.

He said we got to go in early. Sandy is going with us tomorrow. We got back to the room and dropped out of our clothes on the way to the bed. We both crawled under the covers and was almost ready to sleep until Sam realized he needed a little love. I gave him what he wanted. The morning would be here before we knew it.

DAY FIVE

Sandy met us at the plank right off the ship. She was ready and excited to be in Mexico. I was a little tired from dancing last night. Sam was also but caught his second wind, when he saw Carlo waving us down at the street near the port. He was driving a camouflage Hummer. It was sweet. I had never been in a Hummer before.

I had on one of the bathing suits Nan had given me. It was pastel blues and the shoes were the same color. They were like flip flop wedges with material gathered at the toes. The wrap for it was like gauze. It wrapped around your whole body. Different to say the least!

Sam helped me in the truck. He introduces Sandy to Carlo. Carlo helped Sandy in the truck. We were on our way.

Carlo gave us the agenda. He said we were expected at the beach at 2:30pm. They had a 10 a.m. meeting at C&S Mining Company. I looked at the back of Sam's head. What's this, another business meeting?

Carlo was handsome. He wore a linen outfit in a cream color. He was fluent in Spanish and seemed to be mixed race.

It was only 8:45am and it was already warm. I was thinking this must be why Sam has not formally introduced me to Carlo. We were riding about 10 minutes. Sam and Carlo were speaking in English and Spanish. I guess I should have known Sam could speak Spanish but I didn't.

We were passing a strip of stores that was all on one side of the street. I smelled food also. We had not had breakfast. I was looking out of Sandy's window when she and I both saw this store with material waving in the air. She looked at me with a smile and I her. I said, 'Carlo, stop!

We want to look in that store back there with the material.' He smiled and said ok. He turned around and headed back.

Sam commented that this looks like the place he use to bring Nan. Carlo said it was. He pulled up and we got out the truck. Sandy and Carlo seemed shy.

Sam saw a local taco stand and asked me if I wanted a chicken taco. I said yes, but I'm going in this store.

I asked Sandy to come with me. She did. We saw all kinds of beautiful fabric.

The lady in the store was short and plump. She spoke some English though. I got a basket and looked through a few piles of fabric. I saw a dress already made to my left. It was peach with a few other colors. I asked was it for sale. She said yes, si. I told her I wanted it. It seemed perfect. I saw some paisley material that caught my eye. It was unique.

As I moved further into the store, I noticed a dress hanging up high near the register. It was an odd looking pattern. I almost lost my balance when I recognized the pattern. It was Jacob's pattern. I said out loud, Jacob? The lady, who was sitting now, watching us browse, stood up in surprise. She said, 'you know Jacob?' I shook my head. She said Jacob told her I was coming. She said this was my dress. She took it down from hanging high and placed it against me. Sandy said, 'that's hot girl'.

My mouth was still open in shock. My eyes couldn't believe what was before me. The dress was the 'Eternal Love' symbol.

It was amber in color and wow! With the shape I have now, that dress would pop. All my features would show. I was way too shy. I could hardly stop smiling. I wondered what part Sam played. She pulled me by my arm to a table nearby and showed me the 3 inch wedge heels that matched the dress.

There was a scarf made from the same material. 'Fro you try on, I fit.' I unwrapped the gauze sarong and took off my top. Sandy said, 'you have very nice breast, Fro. I bet Sam is having a good time with those.' The lady laughed to herself, out loud. I picked up the dress and found the material a bit stretchy which meant I could put it on over my head. I hurried to do that. I pulled the dress over my head. It went with ease. I pulled it down over my behind and positioned it. I asked the lady what her name was.

She said, 'Mimi'. I smiled thinking you are the bomb, 'Mimi. I asked Sandy if she spoke Spanish. She said yes. I asked her to ask the lady if she made the dress. She asked and the lady answered in Spanish. She said yes. She said she has sown for Nan in the Caymans also. I smiled hard to myself. She came over and checked the dress for fit. There were sheer spots all over the dress but not in the back below the waist and not in the front, in the breast or crotch area. The fit was unbelievable. Jacob said I was gonna introduce his fashion. This dress would do the trick.

I asked if she had anymore that would fit me. Sandy asked her. She said one more. She brought out a sun dress in green and yellow paisley material. I pulled this dress off and tried that one on. It fit really well. I told her I was done for now and wanted to pay her. She said she was coming to the beach party and would bring everything. I took the dress off and put my bathing suit top back on. I asked Sandy if she saw anything she wanted. She held up in the air the dress she liked.

It was a sundress with red in it. She tried it on real quick. It fit the way she liked.

So that's (3) dresses and (1) outfit and the paisley fabric. Mimi asked if I liked the pattern, I said Si. I told her I wanted it in purple and brown fur. She went in the back and came back with two swatches. I had to hold myself. She had a purple swatch and a brown swatch. They were just what I wanted. She told Sandy to tell me she will get the material and when it came in she will take it to Carlo for me. I asked how much money for 3 dresses, 1 outfit and the material. She said $500.00. I gave her the money and we went outside.

Sam and Carlo were standing at the back of the Hummer talking and laughing. It was almost 10 a.m. Sam gave me and Sandy a taco. We ate it with enjoyment. I asked Carlo how he knows Mimi. He said she was his friend's mom. He brings Nan here when she comes with Poppy. He also sends Jacob items to make and sell. I asked Sam if he knew her. He said not really.

I told Carlo she was going to bring 3 dresses and an outfit to the beach party.

Then I formally introduced myself and hugged him. I licked my tongue at Sam. He winked at me.

Carlo started talking to Sandy in Spanish. I got in the truck wondering what meeting this was we were going to next. When everyone was in the truck we left.

We pulled up to C&S Mining Company. Carlo told Sam he was glad he was here for the annual meeting this year. Carlo said he would take us on a tour.

Sam told him we would catch up he wanted to speak with me. He told me this was his and Carlo's business. I said really. He told me that I could not discuss this with anyone, anytime soon. I told him I wouldn't. He said this is one area he wanted my help with. We would be back here soon. Not on vacation. Everything he said seemed cryptic.

We caught up with Sandy and Carlo. The front offices were small and cozy but we went into the back with a key fob.

There were a few people here and there but it looked pretty empty. I saw bins of raw silver.

Carlo said they made bolts and other items using silver. They had a few contracts, was doing well but looking to expand.

I looked around without touching anything. All of a sudden I felt a little faint. I held onto Sam's arm. Then right before my face and directly left was something I never expected to see. It was a diecast. I stopped in my tracks and asked Carlo what was that. He said they used diecast to make lots of bolts. I almost fainted. Sam grabbed me around my waist. He asked was I Okay? I said, 'No Sam!' Die Cast? Really?

I started shouting which startled Sandy and Carlo but not Sam. He knew this was divine revelation. When I came back to myself I was hot and felt overjoyed.

I was in Sam's lap and he was holding on to me tight. He said, 'hey baby, you ok?'

I said, yea! Carlo and Sandy seemed concerned. Sam told them I was okay. I couldn't talk about what was going through my head. GOD was funny. HE set this entire thing up! I was finally convinced. No one could have set this up but GOD!

I knew at that moment that GOD's plan for me was closer than I realized.

Sam hugged me before he released me. He whispered in my ear that he loved me. I kissed him on his cheek knowing we would talk in depth later. I was floating almost.

We went to Carlo's office. There was a glass on the desk. There were 4 glasses and a bottle of Tequila on a tray on the table next to his desk. Envelopes were on the desk also. They were an odd color, I thought. Carlo pulled his chair out for me to sit. He said he didn't know if I needed any, but he will give it to me anyway.

He said that's Sam's experience.

I told Carlo he better stop messing with me. He smiled and told me I was in no position to say anything cause I looked sick a few minutes ago. I said okay, you got jokes.

Sandy jumped in to defend me. She told Carlo he needed to lighten up. This was a first impression. She said, 'Fro is dating yo boi now. Didn't you see the video?'

I looked at Sandy and laughed out loud. I told her if he hadn't seen it before, he sure would now.

Carlo smiled and said he had already seen it. That's why she and I were allowed at their business meeting. Sam finally chimed in. He said Fro was coming to this meeting even if that had not happened.

He looked at Carlo and told him, 'this is HER man.' GOD sent Fro my way and I'm keeping her. I want her. Carlo softened and said, 'I know man!' He told Sam he knew he would find me. Sam told me Carlo was with him the day he took my picture.

I told Carlo I'm sorry he had to put up with him all this time. Carlo thanked me for the sympathy.

Carlo said I call this annual meeting of C&S Mining to order. Sandy leaned against the table. Sam leaned on the desk. The books have been audited. The annual information regarding our company was analyzed. We are in the black for this year. Sam gave a loud woot. Sandy and I smiled at him being silly. Carlo said there are 3 envelopes with our yearly profit divided by three. As per the bylaws the company gets a third to go to the asset line.

Sam and Carlo each receives a third. He picked the envelopes up and asked Sam for prayer. Sam chimed in as if on cue.

'Thank you so much GOD for blessing and keeping us. Words can't express what our hearts feel, knowing that you care for us so much. You allow us to be the head and not the tail. We will never forget nor will we ever get tired of serving you, in Jesus name.' All of us said, 'Amen'.

Sam turned to Sandy and told her that he considers her a friend and he doesn't trust many people but he wants to trust her. He said he would not have trusted her to meet his friend if he thought she would run around telling his private business even though his position is pretty public. He told her he found the woman of his dreams and he would always be connected to me. He said he wanted to include her but had to know he could trust her. She said, 'Sam, I feel you and I agree but I would not betray your trust, ever!' She said she knows GOD has a plan for him and me.

She wants to be around to see it with her own eyes. She was thankful to meet his true friends. She looked at Carlo. Carlo was feeling the heat on him. He said enough of that boi.

He handed Sam an envelope and put one in his pocket. He said since they all say the same thing except for the name, he would read the one for the company. He reminded Sam that he doesn't know how much it is. He opened it and smiled. He said man we share 10 million dollars equally. Carlo gave a loud woot! He and Sam high fived each other.

Sandy and I clapped. Carlo poured Tequila in the shot glasses on the table. When he gave me mine, he said 'Fro, can you handle this? I said, 'sure'. He gave Sandy and Sam a glass. We all said cheers and drank the shot with no back. I thought I felt a hair rise up on my chest. That was strong. Considering I don't drink Tequila.

Sam came over to me and bent down to kiss me. He said I am going to do something different this year. He looked around on the desk for a pen.

Carlo said no man but Sam ignored him. He took his envelope out and wrote on it.
He said, I Samuel Maxwell being of sound mind and body, give this 3.3 million dollars to Frozine. I shook my head. He called Carlo over to initial his statement and asked Sandy to second. He turned to me and smiled just before he kissed me. He searched for my tongue and massaged it softly with his. He kissed my lips and told me I was worth more than money to him. He said he didn't care how I spent it. He wanted me to let him love me. I said okay. He pulled me up from the chair and hugged me. It was only 11:00 a.m.
Carlo said we had to make it to the house because we had company to greet and we had to be at the beach no later than 3 pm. We rolled out and within 10 minutes we were pulling into another gated yard. The house was 2 story and wide. It had a stone exterior. There were cars on the side of the street and in the yard. We pulled near the back.
Carlo told Sam this was his. He did it last year.

Besides they want to see Sam. Sam said, 'I got you'. He told me to stay close to him because he needed me to.

I looked at the house longing for some alone time. Sam said he would show me the house when we finished.

He said, 'Fro these people work for us, be nice.' I said okay. He gave a short speech in Spanish. Then he said something that everyone clapped for. I clapped too. Sam looked at me and laughed. 'What you clapping for?' he asked. I'm keeping the flies away. He looked away with a smile. He must have said something about me because they were looking at me now. He told them I was his woman and he was glad to have me. He told me we would go in shortly. I said, 'Baby I want to sit down, it's hot.' He said, 'No, not yet!' I poked my mouth out, and laughed. He said, 'I'm warning you to be good and stay near me.' I looked for Carlo and Sandy. They were nowhere to be sited. I figured Carlo was hitting that or Sandy was. Sam moved deeper into the back yard walking and talking to those that wanted to talk with him. He made it a point to talk with the older men and women first.

He then made his way to the younger men and women. I tried to sneak off when he turned but he caught me and led me back to where we were standing. This time he held my hand. We met one older lady sitting in a chair. Sam introduced me by name and told her, this is her. She spoke English well. She said, 'I'm happy for you Mr. Max. GOD always looks out for those that look out for others'. She reached out to hug me. I was touched and hugged her also.

When we turned around, almost everyone was gone. Sam led me back to the house. It was after 12 noon. He moved inside and pulled me in. He pushed me up against the wall, reached down and kissed me. It was passionate.

We went upstairs and to the right side. He opened the door to a large room. Even though the room was large, it was partitioned off. I sat in the first chair I saw and took off my shoes and the swimsuit wrap. Sam suggested we take a shower. I said okay. He opened the door to the bathroom area and my mouth dropped. Before us was a 10-15 ft odd shaped Plexiglas clear wall shower cylinder.

There was a bench that looked like the bench you lift weights on, in the small end and rain forest shower head on the opposite end. On the side was a hot tub with bubbling water already in it. Without Sam's permission I went straight to the hot tub, took off my bathing suit and got in. It felt so good. Sam just watched me smiling. I closed my eyes as the jets sprayed water on my body. When I opened my eyes, Sam was sitting on the edge of the bench where water was being sprayed on him.

I commented out loud that this was so cool. He didn't say anything. I got really bubbled up then got out to go to the rain forest shower head area. I stood there and allowed the water to run over my head and body.

My back was turned to Sam. When I turned around, I bent down to allow water to roll off my back and down my legs.

When I looked up, Sam was looking at me. He asked me why I came into his space without permission. I said. 'huh?'. He said, 'you heard me.' I said, 'I don't know who you talking to boi.' He smiled and I could feel he was about to reach for me.

I opened the door and tried to run but he caught me. We were both nude. His little friend wasn't so little right now. I said, 'Sam, wait. We need to talk.' He said, 'I told you to be good but you been being bad.' He forced me to the bench he had been sitting on. He laid me down and straddled me with his body. He held me down because I was trying to get up. I kept saying 'stop playin boi'. He kissed my lips and quickly moved to my breast. He sucked and pulled each one. I yelled in pleasure and pain. He started going further down, past my belly.

When he got down so far, he looked up at me and said, 'every time you are bad, I'm gonna handle you this way.' He licked my soft spot and I yelled again. He turned and saw the cylinder door was opened and closed it with his foot. He went back to her. He sucked and licked gently and then fast. He stuck his tongue almost inside and kissed her. I screamed with passion and he lifted me higher. He went so deep it felt like I was having an out of body experience. All of a sudden I heard the voice again. It was still and small but powerful.

'It's ME child. There are those that need a touch to heal their body and mind. You are being given the gift of Healing! Don't abuse the privilege my child.'

'Also my son, you will be given the power to speak to her and she hears you without verbal words. I love you my children and am allowing you the opportunity to pleasure each other.'

I felt myself coming back and Sam was really enjoying hearing me scream. I was squirming. He stopped and looked at me while he licked his lips. I told him that wasn't right. He said yes it is. He finally let me up. I was soaking wet and trying to hurry out before he changed his mind. When I reached for the handle he put his hand on mine and with no verbal words he said, I want you now. I let out a deep breath and responded okay. He let my hand go and once my feet hit the dry floor, I ran. He caught me. I laughed. He picked me up from behind and carried me to the bed, his bed. He laid me down on my stomach and took me from behind. It felt so good. He pushed in and out for what felt like a long time. Slow with sideways movement then fast strokes.

He found my spot and pressed it hard til I screamed. He slowly withdrew and turned me over. He kissed me passionately again and rubbed my breast til I moaned.

It felt like his little friend moved to my soft spot on its own. Before I could say anything he was back inside and stroking like it was the beginning. He ran across my spot and rubbed it softly. I moaned loudly. He was making love with me at that moment. It was so awesome to be in this position with someone I have the same feeling for. He came long and hard. He sprayed my spot which made me come again too. Then the cool down, slow movements! I truly enjoyed this time. He started to get soft and pulled out. What a session that was I thought. The time was now 2pm. We had 30 minutes to an hour. We decided to rinse off in the rain forest and put our bathing suits back on. We went down stairs to see where Carlo and Sandy were.

Sam knew Carlo wouldn't hurt Sandy so he was comfortable leaving her with him. Not that he wouldn't screw her given the opportunity but he wouldn't force himself if she didn't want to. He had plenty of women who loved Carlo.

Sandy would have to work to win his heart, if she wanted him.

Sam said we were going to a concert on the beach, just for us, but others could come also. Sandy and Carlo came in from outside.

He said 'finally, you two got that out. We heard Fro scream.' Carlo said he told Sandy that Sam went all in and I was officially Sam's woman. I smiled and Sam came up from behind and hugged me.

We left for the beach. We were at Paradise beach. There is an outdoor / indoor club setting. We were out on wood floors. It was like a deck with a top. We sat at a table. The waitress asked what we wanted. I asked Carlo to order for us.

He ordered a Dos Equis and a chicken taco for all of us. It was very good.

I saw some of the soro's in the distance. They were on the beach laughing and playing around. Out of nowhere come Santana and Kem. They started playing and people gathered when they heard the music. I put my head down and smiled hard to myself. I had told Sam I really like Kem's music but Santana is awesome too.

They dedicated a song to me and Sam and new found, true love. We danced. Some of the beach goers from the ship danced too. It was so, so nice. After about 10 songs between them, it was over.

Sam introduced me to Santana first. I hugged him and said, 'bless you baby, I pray GOD heals you'. I hugged Kem too and blessed him to be healed also. Santana was over near the table shaking his arm. He told us his arm has not been this pain free in years. Kem said he felt new as well.

They thanked me for asking for a healing for them. It was 4:30 pm.

Sam and I wanted to get in the water for a little while. Carlo and Sandy went for a walk. Sam and I played like kids in the water. I knew I was going to have to learn how to swim better or this man might accidentally drown me. He splashed me and said never. That will never happen. There was a big artificial iceberg further out in the water. He asked if I wanted to go. It was in deep water. He said I will hold you. You will not only be okay and have to trust me, you will have fun. I agreed.

We moved out further with him holding me up until we got to the iceberg. Of course I was thinking of what fish was below and ready to bite me. We climbed up the iceberg. Sam gave me instructions when I sat in his lap. He said, 'hold your breath once we hit the water.' We went down, my stomach dropped like it would on a roller coaster.

We went down in the water. Sam held me around my waist. We came back up and he let me float on my back with his help until we could stand up. I swam closer to shore, but didn't get out. He went back for a climb on his own. He finally joined me.

We were ready to go back to the ship. When we got back to the outdoor club, we saw Mimi sitting on the steps waiting for us. She had a few bags. Carlo and Sandy were drinking a beer at the bar. Sandy held her bag up and smiled. I gave her thumbs up.

I said 'Hola' to Mimi. She repeated it back. Sam asked her for her hand. He kissed it, she smiled a bashful smile. She handed me two bags. One had the outfit from Jacob. I handed it to Sam. The other was my two dresses and material.

Sam took the dress from the bag, he laughed out loud. He said that boi was something else. He smiled with teeth and looked at me. I shook my head. Mimi must have thought we were talking about her work. She chimed in that Jacob told her to make the dress like this for Fro. Sam told her, no, we weren't laughing at the dress. It is beautiful and well made. We were laughing because Jacob told Fro, she was gonna model his first piece but she didn't know it would be now. She said Jacob was something else. They spoke in Spanish. Sam told me what they said.

Mimi asked Sam to tell me she was giving me
some of the money back.

She said Jacob already paid for the outfit he
ordered for me. I told him to tell her, No.
She is getting material for me. I might have
to ask her to make what I want. She said she
would be happy to.

I hugged her and blessed her health. She
cried and said Bless You, Fro. She hugged me
again and Sam also.

We left for the ship. Sandy sat in the back
with me. Sam and Carlo talked up front. We
looked at our dresses again. We got to the
port at 5:15 pm. Just in time to board.

Carlo told Sam he would see him in a few
weeks. He took Sandy to the side where they
spoke softly. Sam hugged me.

I said, 'you are something else Mr. Maxwell.'
He said, 'touché, Fro.' We started walking
toward the gate to show our ship cards.

Sandy caught up. She hugged me tight. I
asked her what was that for?

She said Carlo sent it to me. He was so busy
making sure she was able to contact him that
saying goodbye slipped his tongue.

I told her thanks but I will get him next time. Sam said Oh No.

We boarded the ship but didn't have to declare our dresses. Sam asked Sandy was 7pm okay since we're just boarding. Sandy said that was good because she needed to rest too. We made it back to our room. I dropped the bags and fell on the bed.

My head was full. The day had been unforgettable. I still couldn't think about it or talk about it yet. I turned over to look at him. 'So you are the truth huh? ', I asked. He asked what did I think? He said no one outside of his island family knows what I know about him. I asked him was he testing me? He said, 'I told you not to do that, Fro.' I said, 'what?'

He said, 'What you just did! I asked you a question and you ignored it and went on to something else.' I chuckled and shook my head. I told him I thought that was a rhetorical question. He said, 'no you didn't.' He told me 'that' has its place and time but it wasn't with him. He said he is all in the conversation and doesn't miss much.

He is getting to know me and he understands I am holding back because I'm afraid of wasting my time or that he might be using me in a way I don't want to be. He said he promises me it is not like that. Yes, he said I need you in my life and I will not let you dismiss me. GOD sent you and I'm ready. You would be too if you let go and be yourself and trust me.
I stopped him because it seemed he was getting too serious. I didn't want to feel threatened by him. The wall would go up and I wouldn't be able to call it, when it would be able to come down. I said okay!
I will answer you. My mind is so full right now my answer may change tomorrow but if you want me to answer, I think your life is unbelievable.
You have been fortunate to be blessed anyway. I wouldn't tell anyone if I were you either. The woman I told would have to be my ace. I would have to know she was or be confirmed by GOD! I was! I'm not going back on my word Sam. I want to date you when we get back home also. I do appreciate you calling me out on my habit or defense mechanism.

It's actually nice to know, that you know I do have the ability to defend myself. I think you should be a little more flexible when it comes to that. It's okay for you to remind me but don't do it to the point that it sounds like you threatening me. I understand your talents and gifts and I know that has to be a heavy burden. But I don't want you to make me afraid of you. You have power.

I'm sure there is other stuff I don't know about yet. But I will fight yo ass back if I have to.

He softened his stare. He was sitting on the balcony watching me on the bed.

He leaned back and lit his cigar. He took a long pull. I rolled off the bed and walked out to the balcony. I had picked up a joint on the way out. I sat on his lap and lit it. I had a flash back. I puff, puff passed. He took it and puff, puff, puff passed. We both laughed out loud again. I turned to face him and said, 'hey playa! I asked you if you were the truth first. You never answered me either. He said, 'my bad, Fro, don't let me screw this up!'

I told him that wasn't my call.

He held me close and whispered that it was more up to me than I knew. I was high now and didn't want to go too deep with this conversation knowing in advance I would get lost. He took another hit of the joint and I finished it.

Sam rinsed the sand off first. I went second. We made our way to the spa deck. Sandy was waiting for me. Sam went in for his massage. I was ready to have the sand rinsed out of my hair. She washed it three times and put the condition on it. She gave me a back massage while we waited. She told me what she thought of Carlo. He was hot but there were women who kept him satisfied. He told her he would like to be like Sam one day, with finding his soul mate. He told her he would fund her idea to be a salon owner. I almost forgot the business meeting. Was he going to do this just for her or he wanted something back. She said he didn't say she had to pay him back but she knows she would one day. I told her if you feel uncomfortable with the offer, let me know and we can work something out without strings maybe. Wonder if she would like to carry a baby for Sam and I?

I knew Sam heard me. He said not now, baby! Let's table that.

I responded okay knowing he heard me. We washed out the conditioner and decided how to wear this hair.

Sandy came up with curls that would pop the new dress we bought. I agreed. Nice for a photo shoot! Sam came over and waited for me. Before long we were on our way back to the room to get dressed for dinner.

When I put on my dress he said, 'you're not wearing Jacob's dress?' I answered no, not tonight. Maybe tomorrow! He also loved the one I had on. It was subtle and sexy. My breast really was wearing this dress. Got to keep them happy! Dinner was fun. It didn't help that we had the munchies. I felt really good and relaxed. Sam was good company. We laughed a lot. We talked a little about the day but I was determined to table that one at least for tonight. He held my hand and played with my fingers.

He had large strong hands but gentle at the same time. His nails were manicured and cut low. He ran his fingers across the top of my dress.

He said my breasts were looking really good in that sun dress. He wore off white. The outfit looked like linen. He said he had the porter iron his outfits. I told him he was a nice dresser. I liked his style. He said Thanks! He said he could hardly wait to see what Jacob hooked up. He laughed and said that boi is something else. I agreed.

I asked how he kept up with Patwa. He said it's the first language he knew. He learned Spanish during his visits with Nan and Poppy. He learned English better when he came to stay with his father. He said he loves the Caribbean. It gives him great pleasure giving back to the people. That's why no one bothers him. None of his businesses have ever been robbed. During the hurricanes his home and business aren't badly damaged.

He said they are in strategic locations and facing the right way to minimize damage.

I told him he must be an excellent swimmer. He said yes. I thanked him for taking care of me on that iceberg today. He told me he would not have had it any other way. It was so nice to be able to talk with an interesting man. I really like this dude.

Wonder why it has taken so long to meet him. Guess we weren't ready before.

We left dinner and stopped to take photos. They were hot. We had a kissing photo that was so hot. The one with his hand on my chest above my breast was sexy as hell. I even felt sexy. The positions we posed in were creative. We walked to the club row and stopped in a jazz club. It was nice. We danced for awhile, swaying back and forth and side to side. We were vibing now and it felt good. Was I falling in love? I didn't think I was ready but it sure felt like it.

We left the club and walked up onto the deck. It was a warm night and my hair was blowing in the night air.

We held hands and stopped every once and awhile to kiss or hug. We found a dark corner and he felt me all over. I took advantage and did the same. He pulled one of my breasts out, played with it and sucked it until I felt myself getting wet. He put it back kissed my neck then my lips and searched for my tongue. This time I wrote on his tongue, 'u baby.' He ran his hands down my back to my hips and squeezed gently.

He pulled me close to him pressed my hips against his crotch and his little friend. It woke up and started to rise. This man just made love to me a few hours ago. He wanted more. He was gonna have to work for it. No easy pootae tonight. Tomorrow was a sea day. We could sleep late so there was no rush to let him have it all in one setting.

DAY SIX

We were so tired the next morning that both of us slept in. We were crusty and satisfied. The morning was here, I awoke first. Sam had his leg across mine and his arm over my waist. I could feel his little friend between my legs snuggled up next to her like the guard at a door or a sleeping dog. I smiled.
This man was becoming use to me and I him. I had to admit to myself that it felt good to wake up to a warm body attached to a gorgeous man. My man is who he wants to be. The idea was growing on me more by the day. I knew without a doubt I wanted a sexual relationship even if we had to play love and war. But I knew just like he must have known that there was only so much love and war to be played. Games can be draining.
Always having to push and pull and remind yourself that you don't have to do this.
I had given my word to a higher power than man. The One who loves me more than any normal man and has eternity waiting for those who seek him. I loved GOD so much right now. HE was allowing me a taste of heaven on earth.

What a mighty GOD I serve. I knew I was being protected but also knew the enemy was not far off. I was determined to be the victor in this assignment. But I knew some things were going to be painful. It's this pain that I was afraid of. There had been so much already. It seemed like I was destined to be solo, until recently. Maybe that's why I am not running into this relationship with Sam. It all seems to be too good to be true and we all know the cliché, 'If it sounds too good to be true, it probably isn't true. But I have to qualify this to say, 'unless GOD ordains it.'
It's creating a stretch in my mind to know GOD has spoken to both Sam and I.
HE wants HIS PLAN to go forth and HE's still willing to use me to do it.
I can't believe everything I need, Sam has. He had it all along and has been saving it up for this hour. I wonder if he knows. In the same breath, GOD has promised something to Sam. If he does what GOD wants he will be rewarded also. Having a woman like me in his life is certainly a plus for him.

Once I'm committed to him fully, no one will be able to fully destroy him, I won't allow it and I have GOD's support. But what his reward is, I have no idea. It almost makes me want to take the chance and trust Sam, just so I can be a witness. He has to be around me to give me what GOD requires anyway.

Then again he doesn't. He has given me access to everything I need to start this assignment. I could complete GOD's assignment and play love and war at the same time. Then again, I don't have the energy for that.

Ain't nobody got time for that non-sense. I am anchored with my teenager who has lost her father and can't lose me too. Not before she's ready. GOD has given us 40 years of perfect health. My daughter should be more than ready before then. I wonder what The Father has for her to do. Guess I'll see sooner than later.

I can imagine I'm going to have to deal with a few left over crushes on Sam. Wonder are they warm or cold leftovers? Even though I know Sam knows which they are, I also know he probably wants to see how I handle myself with them.

I hope I can contain myself even if they go there. It would probably be a good idea to handle them like my older children or a customer from work who is going off. Hopefully they have seen the You Tube video and have had time to digest the fact that they will not have anymore, maybes with Sam. I will have to come up with a tactful way of telling them that Sam is the truth that I have had the opportunity to experience and they will never again get a taste of. It would be so awesome, if this was really real...

Sam moved his leg and turned over. He was still asleep. I was glad. Maybe he didn't hear what I was thinking to myself. I hoped not. He looked so peaceful asleep. Looks like he needed this sleep more than me.

I got out of bed, gently and took a long shower. I put more of the tortoise cream on my body. I could feel it tingling. I got back in the shower to rinse off. My body felt great. I put on the lotion and the oil in my vagina area to help with the soreness from last night. I came out of the bathroom refreshed. Sam was still asleep. I tried my best not to wake him.

I found some shorts and a t-shirt from the college. Cee had given me the t-shirt, last year.

My now perky breast didn't need a bra but my nipples were at attention. I would put on a bra when we left the room. I found one of Nan's joints and opened the balcony door to go out, I saw Sam reposition himself. I smoked half of it and put it out. I was relaxed and feeling great in the heat of the gulf.

Sam turned over and faced me. He said, 'hey baby.' I responded, 'hey sleepy head.' He spoke without words. He told me I wore him out. I said no, I didn't. That was you. He smiled and responded that he had been a bit aggressive yesterday. He said with all that happened he was feeling very good. It must have come off as aggression.

He said he was so sleepy, he felt drugged. He asked how long I had been up. I was so happy to hear him say that.

I just responded I took a shower and came out here. I was still sitting on the balcony facing him with the door open.

He got up and came outside.

He was naked. Even though his little friend was soft, he hit Sam's leg and I could hear the sound. I asked him if he got any softer. He said yes a little more. He said he has special underwear with a pocket in the groan area to support his little friend. I was surprised because I never knew that or asked him before.

He asked for the joint. I lit it and puff, puff passed. He smiled and said don't start that up again. He finished it.

While Sam was dressing and getting ready for the day I made sure I knew where my jewelry was and the joints from Jamaica and Nan. I kept them separated.

Nan's were smoother than Michael's. But both were the same size. I still had (8) of Nan's and (7) of Michael's. I started thinking I should have gotten some from Cozumel.

I put the ring Sam gave me, on and admired my finger and hand.

I still had (2) outfits I had not worn, not including the dresses from Cozumel. I pulled Jacobs dress out. I tried it on. Sam walked out of the bathroom and leaned against the wall. He said, 'wow.'

I looked at the alteration Mimi made. It fit me perfectly. I tried on the shoes. They complimented the dress perfectly also. Sam was putting on clothes and shaking his head. He looked at my body in the dress and said, 'Damn Baby, you are wearing that outfit or it's wearing you.' We both laughed.

I told Sam I wasn't comfortable wearing this because it totally complimented my body and I wasn't trying to show it to everybody.

He agreed but said, 'why hide what you got? I'm sorry, what we got! No one's gonna get it but me.' I smiled. He was right.

'I'm not a super model though and I'm shy', I said. His reply made me shut right up. He said I was a beautiful woman with a figure to match. He said I could handle the attention if I really wanted to. I was untapped beauty and Jacob recognized it. That's why he wants to use me to present his, 'Eternal Love', line. Sam said he would be with me so don't be scared. He said, 'by the way, I got us (10) joints from Cozumel. Carlo gave them to me. I forgot to give them to you since you were so excited about the clothes.' I thought that was good. He reached in his pocket and gave me the bag.

It had 10 perfectly rolled joints in it. I could hardly wait to see what it was like.

I took the dress off and put on a bra with my t-shirt and shorts. We left the room after everything was locked up.

After we found food and ate, we went up top to play putt putt. It was fun. We found seats on the upper deck. The soro's and frat's were on the lower deck taking group shots. It must have been several hundred of them. I didn't know it was that many. We watched them and the others on the deck that were in the hot tubs and pool. Sam told me that there are a lot of people that are lonely and confused. He could hear them. He said the brother that was interested in me was lonely but successful in business. Kind of like Sam was before me. He said he would pray that GOD is as good to the brother as HE had been to himself.

He said several of the soro women had been diagnosed with breast cancer. They were on this cruise for rest and were gathering strength for the fight. He said one of the women was the woman who wouldn't ask him if he loved me. I was so touched. I asked Sam to point the other woman out to me.

He did. I made a mental note to speak and pray with them.

He said there were a few of the brothers who had cancer also. Some were plagued with painful past injuries and were sad because of it.

I made Sam point them out to me also. I was happy to be part of bringing new found relief to these people. After all they were a part of my new found experience.

Sam reached over and kissed me. It was so passionate I forgot for a moment that we were outside.

A couple came over and sat in the chairs in front of us. The guy turned around, introduced himself, and then addressed Coach. He asked Sam if he was really the UVA Coach. Sam asked him why he wanted to know. Even though Sam already knew, the guy said he use to attend the school and followed them even now.

He said there was a lady that worked in his office who has Sam's picture on her desk and said she was dating Sam exclusively. He said she comes across as a little off and he wanted Sam to know.

He said he knows Sam is dating me and he has seen that we are serious, so the woman has to be delusional.

He said we seem to be a perfect match and he didn't want to see anything happen to Coach or me. Sam told him that was nice of him to be concerned for our safety. He said he supports the school and doesn't want anything to happen. Sam asked him what the lady's name was. He paused and said he wasn't trying to get her in trouble. Sam told him he would never reveal his name or affiliation to the woman. Sam knew already but wanted me to hear. He said her name is Jennifer Redd. Sam reached for his hand, the man extended his. They shook on it.

He told us, it was nice to meet us, especially on a cruise with him and his new wife.

I smiled and said congrats. I asked the lady her name. She smiled and said Cathy. I smiled and said, Fro.' They got up and said they were going to get ready for dinner early because the comedy show was at 7p.m. and 10 p.m. They were catching the 7 p.m. show. We said we would see them around.

I looked at Sam and shook my head. 'Really?' I said. He told me he knew she was trying to meet him. He knew her name was Jennifer but he didn't care to know anything else about her. I asked him was that the lady the Coaches were talking about? He said yes. He said he thinks she has a fatal attraction toward him. He was not going to entertain her at all.
I told him it would be okay. I will beat her ass. He said, 'no baby.' I said if she steps to me and shows any part of her ass, I will do just that. He said the woman was rejected by someone who he reminded her of.
I said, 'so, she needs a healing?' He said, 'yes'. I said okay and if that doesn't work can I beat her ass then? He shook his head. I thought to myself, this is one of the reasons he needs me.
How can he concentrate on the team if he's constantly running from a crazy woman?
I would help him with this even if we weren't dating. He said, 'thanks Fro.' I said, 'No problem, Sam.' So now it starts. I knew it wasn't gonna be easy.

He looked at me with tears almost. He said, 'Fro, it's not my fault women like me for whatever their reason is. I couldn't be with them without consequences and I have way too much to lose.

GOD sent you to help me too baby. HE knew it had to be you. I was so tired of the roller coaster and like you, I was ready to give up until I saw you.

I have been preparing for you to be part of my life.

You satisfy my hunger for love on all levels and I know your heart can protect mine just like mine can protect you. I really want you and need you in my life. We have consummated our love, you know that. I know you had to be there when I broke you off. Wait, you were passed out.'

He was trying to make light of the situation. He said, 'Fro, it's gonna pass. You are very good at what you do and I am in your corner 100%.' The more I thought about it, the calmer I became.

There was no way I would allow a woman or man to get away with threatening me, which would spill over to my baby girl.

Sam said, 'exactly!' Music started playing which caught our attention. It was almost time for our massage. I got up and stretched. Sam looked me up and down and smiled.
I knew he was seeing me in that dress.
We went back to the room, undressed and put on our robes.
We were on the spa deck in no time. Sandy said wow you two are on time. When Sam left, I said, 'girl he is makin me wear that dress.' She said, 'that dress is hot. You will be receiving a lot of attention. Make sure you go to the bathroom before you go to the show.' She said she had something special for that dress. My hair was continuing to grow to the point I was concerned my daughter would think I got weave. My hair was curly with red hi-lites and so rich. Sandy gave me an up/down look. One side was up and pinned back. The other side was down and spiral curled. I really liked it. I finished early and peeped in on Sam. Two little ladies were massaging his feet and back. He had on his underwear and a towel over his middle.
I closed the door back and told Sandy to tell Sam I had gone back to the room.

He heard me and said I know what you doin to get your nerves together.

He asked me to wait for him. I told Sandy maybe I should wait for him, he's always waiting for me. She agreed.

We chit chatted about things. I asked if she was going to Key West tomorrow, she said no. She had booked five Sorority sisters since it was the last night. She said she was giving me a mohawk so I had to be there at 6p.m. She said the ship wasn't leaving Key West until 10 p.m. since it was US Territory. I told her I would be there. I've always wanted a Mohawk. Sam walked up and spoke to Sandy before we left.

When we got back to the room, I put on a shower cap and found a Cozumel joint. We went out on the balcony to smoke. Sam lit his cigar and I the Cozumel special. It was even smoother than Nan's and it didn't smell so loud.

After puff, puff no pass. I felt it right away. I puff, puff, puff no pass again.

I was straight. Sam asked if I was gonna share. I gave him the remainder and went to shower.

I took a quick shower since we hadn't been anywhere much today, nor had we been in the water.

When I came out Sam was still on the balcony. He was looking out at the water, the sun had already set.

He turned to me and his eyes were blood shot like he had been crying. He said he knew about his eyes. He was a little emotional because he was thinking about his mom. He said she would love me and him together. I stepped out and hugged him. I kissed him passionately.

'Come on and get ready so we can eat and get a good seat.' I said. He smiled. 'Anything you say if I can just feel your behind in that dress.' I ignored him.

I put the dress on without a bra and had on no-line underwear. I didn't wear thongs.

Sam came out of the bathroom and took one look at me and said no! Your nipples are too inviting. Someone might want a lick. I took the dress off and put on a strapless bra. It looked great even to me. My body was feeling great.

Sam wore navy blue. It complimented the dress very well. His top two buttons were not buttoned. He sure did look sexy. I was becoming heated. He liked my hair with the dress. We went to dinner and got a lot of head nods. We ate light and left early to take special photos. I took a few alone for Jacob and his portfolio. The photographer was advised he was taking the first photos of this design. He did an exceptional job.

People were stopping to look and took their own photos. Sam and I looked like a perfect couple. I knew this would be on You Tube also. Everywhere Sam put his hands on me was the mesh. He was even surprised.

I took the last photo facing Sam and reaching up on my tip toes to kiss him. My behind was in plain view and where Sam had his hand was mesh. That Jacob!

We entered the comedy show before it started. We were lucky to find a seat in the middle. It was a love seat and it was yellow. I smiled. I asked him to get me a drink from the bar. When he came back he didn't have enough mixer in the drink. He told me to go get it.

I laughed because I knew what he was doing. There weren't a lot of people seated yet so I got up walked off and looked back, Sam had his legs crossed and was smiling, looking at me. I licked my tongue and walked on. I got more cherries and additives.

Sam watched me walk back. I walked slower and sexier. There was music playing. I stood still and danced in place before I got back to my seat. I was feeling really good.

He laughed at me. He told me he knew I would be okay with the dress.

The soro's and frat's started filling the right side of the room. They were rolling deep too. Sam and I talked and played around while we watched people at the same time. The show would start in 10 minutes.

I forgot to do what Sandy told me to do. I had finished the drink and had to pee. Sam really laughed now. I felt really shy because he was laughing and the Greeks were pouring in.

Once I stopped laughing myself, I hit Sam who put his hands up continuing to laugh. I got up, straightened out my dress and walked towards the door. I pretended they weren't there.

They stopped talking when I got close and they got a look at my body in that dress. There were cat calls and a lot of 'damns'. I looked at the group as a whole and smiled but I caught the eye of Charles. He smiled seductively. I blushed and nodded to him. He licked his lips, I walked out.

I made it to the bathroom and relieved myself. The women in the bathroom looked at the dress. Some wanted to touch it. They wanted to know where I got it. I told them in Cozumel at a small village shop. They said they really liked it. The two ladies I needed to speak to came in the bathroom. They were kind of sad but talking with each other.

I saw the large stall was empty. I opened the door and asked them in. They went in and I went behind them and locked the door. They looked at each other then at me and the dress. I ignored their stare and got to the point.

I told them that I wanted to pray a healing prayer with them.

I said I don't know exactly what's wrong but something is. Tears filled their eyes.

We held hands and I prayed for GOD to forgive us and asked for a miracle of healing of our bodies. I said we will forever be grateful and we will never forget it was you GOD that healed us this day. Amen. They both said Amen.

I put my hands on the first girls chest. She cried. I put my hand on the back of the other girl and my other hand directly on her breast. She jumped.

I told her I wasn't gay nor did I get down with women. I told them I loved Sam. This woman began to cry also.

They leaned on the wall of the stall and got themselves together. I got toilet tissue and wiped their eyes and faces. Each one hugged me. The one who hollered at Sam gave me an extra hug and apologized. I told her that was okay.

I said, 'Sam is fine girl, but he's officially taken, by me and I'm not giving him back nor am I sharing.' She shook her head in agreement. I said, 'he does love me.'

We left the stall. I washed my hands and left them in the bathroom.

I walked back in the club and stopped right in front of Charles. I turned and looked at Sam who was looking at me smiling.

I turned all the way around and danced in place for a moment. I swayed my hips back and forth and did a 2 step. Charles laughed out loud.

I walked back to my seat. Sam clapped. He said, 'you bad baby.' I said, 'You are making me that way.' We both laughed.

The show was great. We all went to the club and partied after the comedy show. Sam and I only danced with each other. When we were ready to leave, Sam pointed out the guys who had cancer and prolonged pain from injuries. I went over to each of them and asked them to meet me outside they complied. I told them Somebody asked me to pray for their healing. They seemed touched. We held hands and I prayed. I touched each of them in their chest. We counted it done. Sam and I went back to our room. We were already still high so we undressed and made out on the balcony before coming inside to bed.

He kissed me from head to toes. He laid on his back and said, 'you were wonderful tonight.

You handled your business with the soro's and frat's.

I saw your little show you performed in front of them and him. I knew you could do it, if you wanted to. Can I have the same show?' he asked. I laughed out loud. I told him he was jealous. He said, 'yes, I am'. I repositioned myself and got on top of him. I kissed him long and sucked his tongue til he moaned either in pain or pleasure.

I started moving around on top of him til I felt his little friend. I found his little friend and guided him inside. I got up and sat on his penis. It filled me up. He moaned. So did I. I started doing the same dance I did in front of the Greeks. I put my back into it when I stood up on my knees. I slowly got in a crouch position and went up and down his little friend like it was a real pole. He said, 'wait baby, wait a minute.' I said, 'no'! I wanted him right where he was. I leaned back and slammed into him. He said, 'oh baby wait'. I said, 'no'. I rode his little friend like he was a horse and I was the rider. Wish I had a whip to finish the job. He said, 'no baby, just you.' He yelled that he was coming. He did.

DAY SEVEN

The last day of the cruise ported in Key West. The stay would be extended. We slept late since we were up til 2a.m. or so. I had to admit this was some vacation. My life would never be the same after we got back home, I was sure of it.

Sam got up first this time. I felt lazy but he opened the balcony door. It was hot in Key West.

I got up and finished in the bathroom. He said I should wear shorts and shoes that held my feet in. I found shorts and gladiator sandals. I wore a bathing suit top. It was one that Nan gave me. I joined him on the balcony and took a few puff, puff, puff passes from Sam. He said he had plans and we had to get going. I took a joint with me just in case. He said we would eat well. We left the ship after we locked everything up.

When we got to an inner city location, Sam waved down a cab. He said, 'Hilo pad, man!' The cab driver asked which one. He said the closest. When we got there, there was a helicopter waiting.

I looked at Sam thinking huh, I'm not going on that over the water. He said it was better over the water. I told him I was scared. He said, 'I got you. If anything happens, I will take care of you.' I said, 'you promise?' He said yes. So I got on the helicopter and Sam told the pilot, Key Largo.

We put on ear phones due to the noise. I held onto Sam's arm. It was scary but nice. He said it was faster this way than driving. I wondered where we were going but chose to allow the surprise.

He told me without words that there was a nice restaurant he wanted me to try their food. He said the view was nice also. We had not had breakfast and I was getting hungry. The copter shook a little too much for me. Sam told the pilot to do something in technical terms I did not understand.

He did. He said, 'thanks man'. 'You fly?' Sam looked at me but was talking to the pilot. He said, 'yes' I looked at him hard. 'What the hell?' I was thinking. Sam said, 'yeah Fro, I fly! I have a plane, well it's a jet.'

I smiled hard and said to myself, 'Who the hell is this man?'

Fro, what have you gotten yourself into? Sam looked at me and said without words that he was my new man who was more than capable of taking care of me. He said he needed me to feel the same about him.

I thought we will talk! We have a lot to discuss. This vacation isn't over yet.

I said to Sam that he needs to keep an eye on the sky, road. He laughed. We finally arrived at the Hilo pad. I saw a group of shops in the distance.

He paid the guy and said we would need a ride back in 3 or 4 hours. He paid the guy an undisclosed amount of money. I asked how much but he refused to tell me.

We walked down the street holding hands. We talked and laughed. He told me the restaurant had very good tilapia and crabmeat, sweet potato sticks and a surprise dish. My mouth was watering now.

I didn't ask him how he knew of this place but did ask who he brought to eat here. He said he brought this woman a few years ago. I asked what happen to her.

He said she was shallow, loud and not his type even if she could handle his little friend which she could not.

We got to the restaurant and went in. It was quaint but nice. The waitress was a young woman with dirty blond hair. Her name is April. Sam ordered for us. He asked for a beer for each of us. They had Dos Equis. I liked this place already.

They finally brought our food out. It was hot and smelled great.

The fish was good, so was the crabmeat then I spied the sweet potato stick and some delicious looking plantains. They were right on time. They even tasted better than Nan's but I would never tell her that.

Sam watched me eat with my eyes closed. He laughed and called me silly. Then the waitress came back with a basket. It was coco muffins with honey butter. I laid my head on Sam's shoulder and rubbed his chest. They were very, very good.

The waitress came over and smiled. She said, 'they good right?' I said, 'yes Lord, they are.' She smiled. We had a large plate of food and both of us ate off of it.

I fed Sam and he fed me. This was worth the helicopter trip. The lemonade / tea was off the chain. Just as I was feeding Sam some crabmeat, I heard a woman's voice.

He said, 'damn! Not her.' I looked over by the door and saw this very pretty woman who was dressed very cute. She looked over at us and said, ' I know he didn't bring another bitch to our spot.' Sam said, 'Sara.' He told me without words that she was the woman he brought here to eat. He said he had no idea she was here.

She came over from the front counter. The waitress looked distressed. She stepped in front of us and looked at us one at a time. She asked Sam why he has not returned her calls. She said it had been two years and now he shows up here with this bitch. I saw **red** all of a sudden. Sam held my arm and squeezed it to get my attention. He said without words that she was unworthy of the ass kicking I could easily provide her with. I ignored him because there was something I knew that Sam didn't know about women.

I swallowed my food, put my fork down and picked up the knife.

I stood up and moved from behind the table without a word. Sara backed up, a bit.
The few people that were sitting at their table stopped eating.
I held the knife in both my hands and without yelling I told her, I was not her bitch or Sam's and if she disrespects me one more time she would regret stepping her ass in that door. I asked her if she heard what I said. She looked at me and sucked her teeth like a child. She looked at Sam, like help me out here. Sam shook his head.
He said, 'Fro baby, this is Sara. We went on a few dates a few years ago but it didn't work out.'
She looked at Sam and asked him why he had not returned her calls. She acted like she didn't hear what he said. She told him she had waited for him and found a place in Key Largo to live.
She thought he was busy and would come back for her.
I could see this woman was confused and it was gonna take Sam to break it down for her.
I moved away from her and put the knife on the table.

The waitress came over and asked if everything was alright. She looked at me almost sad. I told her just a moment. I bent down and picked up my side purse, kissed Sam on his lips and said I was gonna go to the bathroom.

I told him but looked at the woman and said, 'that's how much time you have to talk to her.' Sam said, 'okay.'

I asked the waitress to show me where the restroom was. She smiled and led the way. She opened the door to the restroom and went in first. She kind of startled me but I followed anyway.

She said that woman was the bitch. She treats all the women nasty and is always trying to talk to other women boyfriends or husbands. She said, I should have cut her or beat her up, she would have helped me. April said she was sorry our dinner was messed up. I smiled at her. She asked me if she smoked would I tell. I told her no. She opened the window that looked out on the water and pulled out $\frac{3}{4}$ of a joint. She lit it before I could say anything. She puff, puff passed. I puff, puff, puff passed. She laughed.

We blew the smoke out of the window.
She puff, puff, puff, puff passed and I
finished it and flushed the roach down the
toilet. The buzz was nice but not like mine. I
pulled mine out and puff, puff, puff, puff
passed. She took it and I told her to keep it.
She put it out for later I'm sure.
She said she was gonna put a bag together for
us. She said she saw me chowing down on
those muffins and plantains. I laughed and
told her they were my favorite.
She seemed afraid to ask so I volunteered. I
told her Sam and I were just entering into a
relationship and we just realized we love each
other. I told her I knew women liked him but
I didn't know they were so crazy.
She said, 'you not afraid of leaving him with
her this long.' I responded that he needs to
explain things to her, not me.
I also told her he wouldn't leave me here, for
her. She said, 'right'.
I stood up and reached in my purse for money.
I asked her to bring me another beer, a little
bit of crab meat, a couple of coco muffins and
a few plantains. I gave her a $100.00. She
said, 'you don't have to pay me that much.'

I said, 'I know, but you helped me when I
wanted to cry. This is my way of saying thanks
and good looking out with the puff, puff pass.'
She laughed. We were both high now. I put
on my shades. She laughed again.
I responded they will think I am hiding tears
when I'm really hiding the fact that I'm high.
We both said, 'puff, puff pass' and laughed.
She started out first and said to give her 2
minutes before I left. She stopped and
sprayed air freshener and closed the window.
I left the restroom and walked back to our
table.
Sara was sitting next to Sam and wiping her
eyes. Sam said without speaking, 'are you
okay?' I thought to myself, 'you know I'm
alright.' Sara looked up at me and said she
was sorry for the way she acted and what she
said. She didn't mean to make me cry. I
looked away to keep from laughing. I pointed
to my seat.
She knew what I meant and got up. I sat down
and pushed the plate to the side. April came
right over and picked it up and left me a beer.
I leaned back and took a swallow.
I asked them if they were done.

Sara looked at Sam who looked at me with my shades on and said, 'she knows I love you, Fro.' Just then April brought out my plate. It smelled very good. I got a clean fork and said, 'okay...Did you tell her that I don't fight over a man but if she ever steps to me and calls me a bitch again, especially when she doesn't know me, I will not excuse myself and I will handle my business?' "No, I didn't tell her but you just did.'

I stuck my fork into the crabmeat and put it in my mouth. It was good.

I looked up at Sara who seemed to be waiting for something and said, 'Sara, I love Sam too! I am sorry this didn't work out for you but he is my man now and I'm not giving him back to you or anyone else, ever. I wish you the best in finding a man who loves you too but I know it will never be this man.

Excuse me but this food is great and have you ever tried the coco muffins?'

She walked off without giving a response. I ate a plantain and fed Sam more crabmeat. He reached over and kissed me on the cheek, my mouth was chewing. He took a swallow of my beer and took a bite of the coco muffin.

He smiled and agreed that this combo was tasty.

He put his arms around me and said 'thank goodness for the puff, puff pass.' We both laughed and kissed passionately.

We finished the food. I asked Sam to let me pay and I left another $100.00 on the table. We left the restaurant and I still had on my shades. When we got down the street a block or two, Sam took my shades, looked at me and laughed saying I was something else. I tried to get my shades back but he held them up high.

He said you and that waitress was smoking weren't you. I said 'no baby! I was crying and she wiped my tears.' He said, 'that's not true.' I thought to myself that he knew I wasn't crying and he knew exactly what I was doing but I still don't know what him and Sara talked about. And to be honest, I don't want to know. He handed my shades back and said, 'I want to tell you but I'm so amazed right now. Almost any other woman would have reacted differently to that mess but not you.' He was happy because I told someone other than him, that I loved him.

He said that was the first time and it actually feels good. 'I couldn't believe I said it out loud either. I guess you are growing on me.' We kissed passionately right there on the sidewalk.

We made it back to the Hilo pad where the original man was there waiting for us. Sam helped me up but felt my behind while doing it. I jumped. He smiled seductively.

We were on our way back to Key West with plenty of time to spare. This time there were no problems with the helicopter. I was glad. We stopped at a pub on the route to the ship. Our shipmates were dancing in a soul train line and taking tequila shots. We watched for awhile but did not participate.

We walked back to the ship. We had time to kill so we walked around to find the hot tubs and Jacuzzi's. I told Sam I would like to get in later.

There was going to be a party tonight on the deck. It was the last night.

I had a lot of thoughts to process and many questions to ask Sam.

This had been an overwhelming experience that no one would ever believe because I could hardly believe it myself.

I stopped by the spa deck to talk to Sandy. Sam said he had a few things to do so he left me with Sandy.

She was working on the last head before me. She asked how my day was. I told her it was great but we ran into one of Sam's old dates. Sandy and the lady she was working on wanted to know what happened.

I couldn't tell them everything but I told them how I was tempted to cut the woman but left the table for Sam to correct the situation. They couldn't believe it. They both said they would have jumped the woman. I reminded them that I was just beginning a relationship with him and would not fight a woman over him unless physically provoked. They agreed.

Sandy said plenty of women come in the shop and ask about Sam. He has a lot of admirers. 'The man is downright fine and Fro is trying to decide if she wants to date him.'

I had to admit she had a point but I knew she wouldn't think the same thing if she knew the entire truth as I knew it.

No one would believe it. She said, 'there were a few brothers who came to the shop who were attracted to Sam. They said maybe he wasn't dating a woman because he wanted to date a man and they would be more than willing to help.'

I said, 'wow, they really think he's gay?' She said they did. She said about 5 years ago, before she actually met him there was a rumor that he didn't like women. He spent a lot of time with the football team and some people began talking bad about him and that he shouldn't be around the young men.

It took the players and staff to speak out on his behalf. He started being seen with females sometimes but never too long.

When they became friends a few years ago, she was gonna try to date him but he told her he had seen the woman he wanted and no one else would do. He asked her could they still be friends. He was very nice and would do anything for folks.

He donated equipment and money to local charities. She's never met anyone like him. But he's always been a straight up guy.

He's been friendlier towards people this past year. I asked her was she satisfied being friends in lieu of dating him. She said yes. She wouldn't try to get with someone who was in love with someone else. She believed him because he believed it and she trust him and want him to be able to trust her as a friend. 'Fro, that man is yours honey and he's not gonna be with anybody but you so you might as well get used to it.' I smiled knowing she was right. The lady in the chair asked for a tissue. She was crying. I asked her what was wrong. She said it was so sad how people misjudged Sam. She wished she had a man who searched for her, found her and did all the things he has done for me.

He has to be almost broke when he gets home. She would give anything to find her soul mate. I didn't know what to say because she was only half right. Sam was nowhere near broke.

I told her I was flattered by Sam's advances but I didn't fall for what men or women for that matter, told me. I had not been seeking a relationship when Sam and I met again.

I didn't have any bills and any need for a man to do anything except sex me for the few minutes they were capable of. I told her I had given up on love and decided to concentrate on finishing raising my daughter who graduates from high school next year. She said, 'What about you?' I laughed out loud. 'I had all but given up' I said.

I was tired of the games and men always talking a good game. Sandy chimed in that Sam don't play no games with women. Sandy was really in the Sam, amen corner. Sandy said, 'Fro, you know you love that man and you ain't letting him go either!'

After a moment of looking down, then in the air up high, I told Sandy and the lady yes, I was feeling him and no, I wasn't giving him back to the women and men of this world. Sandy clapped. She said, 'that's my girl.' The lady seemed happy too. She said, 'you make them men and women who made your man feel bad, regret it. Do it for him. He will appreciate having you stand up for him and love him at the same time.' I said, 'yes, he will.' Sandy was finished with the woman's hair. The lady hugged me.

I don't know what made me do it but I hugged
her back and blessed her health. She said
thanks.
Sandy started on me after she walked the
lady out and received her tip.
Sam spoke to me without words. He asked was
I having fun listening to the women tell a small
piece of his history. I told him he should have
told me himself. He said that part is painful
but he would have gotten around to telling me
about it.
Sandy doesn't know the true story herself.
She is repeating rumors because he never told
her. He likes Sandy but she has a habit of
saying things that she shouldn't say aloud.
She really thought she was telling me news.
He asked me to be careful what I reveal to
her. He's still waiting to see if she's going to
repeat the fact that he and Carlo made a 3
million dollar profit at C&S Mining. I almost
forgot that.
I said to him that he doesn't have to worry
because I'm not Sandy. He said, 'no you're not,
you are my woman and I love you and it was
nice hearing you tell them the truth.' I smiled.

Sandy washed my hair and conditioned it. While we waited, she put the shampoo & conditioner in a baggie, gave it to me, saying Sam had asked her to do that the last night of the cruise.

My hair grew almost an inch. It had almost doubled in length since the cruise started. The red hi-lites fit me perfectly. She started braiding my hair on one side and then the other until it met in the middle. She curled the middle. She said it would last a week. That would give me time to get home and unpack before I had to do hair. Even if it got a little wet it would be okay. Sam came in just when we were finishing. He asked if I wanted to get a massage with him. I told him I did. Sam had his checkbook with him and wrote a check to Sandy for styling my hair during the cruise. He gave it to her without allowing me to see it. She looked at it and a tear fell. She hugged him and said Thank You. She thanked me for the opportunity to style and care for my hair. I hugged her and told her I would make it a point to visit her when I came to visit Sam.

She said the pleasure would be hers.

I teased her and said when Sam and I get ready to have a baby, she can help us by carrying it. She laughed and said, 'Sure Fro.' Sam told her to ignore me. She hugged me and we stepped into the room for massages. The two ladies smiled and said, 'Good, you were able to bring her this time.' I took off my clothes got on the table, then put a large towel over my middle and breasts. I told them I want a full massage to include my breast and buttocks.

They agreed. Sam and I laid on the matching tables and looked at each other, smiling, licking our tongues and winking. The massage was very nice and when they finished, I was almost feeling light headed.

Sam said without words that this was a piece of cake compared to what he had in store for me.

I said yeah, right. Bring it, Mr. Maxwell. He laughed out loud and said, 'okay.' We made our way to our room and dressed for dinner. I wore the sun dress from Mimi's shop. It was a cute dress.

Sam wore a green linen suit. He was so handsome. I told him I was honored to be his date tonight.

He smiled and said, 'even though you know you mine after dinner and there will be no backies.'

I laughed and kissed him. Dinner was nice, we said goodbye to our maitred' and Sam gave them additional tips.

The two of them, told us we were a beautiful couple and GOD has blessed us. They wished us well for the future. We took photos and they were very nice. The photographer said he would have them ready at 1 a.m. Sam told him we would come by.

We left and didn't go to the club.

We ordered a drink from the casino and went walking up on the deck.

The ship was preparing to leave Key West.

We found a spot up top and leaned on the rail to watch. We talked about the day. Sam apologized again for Sara. He said he told her she was taking her sadness and pain out on the wrong people.

Even if he had not found me yet, he still would not have dated her.

He told her he knew she only wanted material things and so having sex would have complicated matters more because he knew he wasn't in love with her. She seemed to understand.

He told me there were a few other women who were obsessed with the idea of a relationship with him based on looks and what he did for a job. He knows what they think so he would be a fool to fall for that and he was no fool.

We talked about the cruel thing that happened at the college. He said he couldn't tell them the real reason he didn't have a woman. He didn't want to hurt them. They would have plenty to talk about. He said in no way was he gay but couldn't defend himself without divulging his secret.

No one would understand. He said they still wouldn't. I agreed.

He said that was hurtful because some of his friends began to distance themselves from him. So he was pretty much on his own with GOD's help.

He spent his spare time learning to fly planes. I leaned on the rail and asked him what about me?

He said he really loved me and welcomed me into his life with open arms. He thought GOD must really love me to create you for me. After we finished our drinks we went back to the room to pack. We smoked a little. As I was putting the clothes together a white medium sized box fell out of one of the bags. I didn't recognize it. I asked Sam. He said it was from Jacob.

He said Jacob told him to give it to me when we were on our last day of the cruise. I opened it. It was beige fabric with the eternal love symbol imprinted on it. Jacob wrote the note for my eyes only. I opened it and read it to Sam.

'Fro, by now I know your senses have been thoroughly shocked. It was wonderful to meet my brother's woman. You are that to him and by now he has proved who he is to you.

This fabric is for your wedding dress. I know one day soon, Sam will be your husband and you will belong to me too.

Love Always, Jacob.'

I cried while Sam held me in his arms and cried too. These were tears of, '*hi baby, it's me, where have you been.*' After a few minutes, I put the material in my bag and zipped it up. I left my jewelry in the safe because we had to go back out to see the photos. When we got to the gallery the photographer was waiting for us.

He gave us two albums. There was a duplicate for me. When I started looking through the book I smiled hard. It was very nice.

The guy gave Sam the memory card and each album had a disk or DVD in the inside pocket. Sam watched while he deleted the temp files and any of our photo files from the computer. He also waited for him to empty the trash.

He told him he did not want to see any of these pictures anywhere we did not send them and if so, he knew who to contact. The photographer assured him they were deleted. Sam paid the photographer.

Again he wouldn't tell me how much they cost. We went back to the room and looked at the album. We laid across the bed and went through each day.

It was something to see how I was changing. The photo with Jacob's dress was the best! Sam looked at the photo and shook his head. He reached over and kissed me.

He said he would have large prints made for Jacob and Nan. He would put one up in Cozumel also.

We put all of our things together and was ready to go tomorrow.

He said we may need to stay in Miami for one more night. I said that was good because I wanted to.

I told him I wanted to go out with him. He said okay, but I had to wear Jacob's dress. He said he would hold my hand for comfort. We got undressed and started feeling each other all over. I felt his little friend, his legs, hips, chest, head and moved half way up on his body. I caught his lips and kissed the inside of his mouth. I played with his tongue and kissed the ends of his mouth.

I thought to myself that this man is so sexy to me and I am so enjoying his company. I certainly could get use to this. He said without words that we had at least 40 years to enjoy each other.

He wrapped me up in his arms and turned me over where I was on the bottom. He kissed me and ran his hands through my Mohawk hair style. He said he liked it on me. He kissed my neck, moved down to play with my breast and put them so far in his mouth and sucked. It felt so good. I moaned with pleasure. He moved down my stomach to my mound and beyond. He opened my thighs wider and licked softly as it became rhythmic. I held on to the bed as he kissed my soft spot almost like he kissed my lips. He said it tasted so good. I asked him to let me taste. He crawled backup to me and kissed me so softly. I licked his lips and tasted the sweetness of my excitement. It tasted like an aphrodisiac that I wanted more of. He said it tasted like love to him. He went back for more.

This time he used his lips and kissed the entry like he was kissing my lips.

He stuck his tongue inside and French kissed my soft spot with such passion, I started releasing more and more juice. I held his head and my hands moved as he did.

I let go of my shyness and melted into him as if we were one moving in a dance. Our dance!

He told me without words that he has never felt this way before but he liked it, no, loved it. He said his little friend wanted to participate in the party too. I screamed for him to hold me. I felt like I was losing control of me. He came up to my mouth with juice on his lips. I licked them and we kissed passionately. His little friend found the entrance to my soft spot and slowly pushed his way in. I felt out of body almost. He was extremely hard and it felt like he was leading Sam instead of Sam leading him. Sam squirmed and moaned out loud.

He finally made it all the way inside me and then he pulled back and pushed in and nestled between my legs and said baby, I'm home. He reached down and pushed my hips to him to make sure he was all in. My face was in his chest. His chest hairs were caressing my lips and I found his nipple and nibbled on it.

He held me until I turned my head so his chest massaged my cheek. He moved his hands back up my back and said, 'hold on tight, this ride might get bumpy.'

I was so close to releasing my juice I could hardly keep still.

I put my arms around him and got a good grip. I couldn't lock my arms because he was too thick. He pulled out a short ways and pushed back in. His little friend was so hard I could feel this muscle against my soft spot easily and I got very excited. All of a sudden he pulled back and ran the tip of his penis across my spot. I yelled with pleasure. He started long stroking me. He pulled almost all the way out, moved from side to side and pushed back in all the way. I screamed with passion. Every time he touched my spot I came. Now every time he moved, I moved. He pulled back, I pushed up. I pulled back, he pushed in. We were in rhythm.

It felt like nothing I had ever felt before. It was so juicy because I was in a constant orgasm. He moved faster and faster until we were rocking back and forth and moaning and yelling like we were the only ones on the ship. Sam was sweating and it became harder to hold onto him. I let go and enjoyed the ride. I must have come for 10 minutes.

I was so into this love that I felt myself drift away almost like I was asleep but awake too.

Suddenly it was very quiet. I knew this time what it was.

GOD was talking already and it was like I was far away and the closer I got the better I could hear him. But I wasn't physically moving. **HE asked me if I was a believer now?** I said yes. But why me I asked.

Again HE said because I love you and this man makes you happy. I always wanted you to be happy. You weren't ready before and neither was Sam. Both of you are ready now. I asked ready for what?

He said He wanted us to complete what He asked me to do. He said the people are almost ready.

Sam asked what the people were ready for. This was the first time I heard Sam speak.

GOD said the people were almost ready for Him. They have to know He is not dead but yet alive. He loves those who already know Him and is seeking to bring life to the lost. He said He created Sam as he is and me as I am. Righteous! He said as a couple we were powerful. Alone we just had power. He told Sam not to be afraid because he was near and gave me to him.

He told Sam it was okay to love me. He told me Sam was who he sent and I could always trust him. He told me to stand up for Sam when it was needed and Sam was to do the same. He finally said, I AM has given you all you need to take my message forward. He said our seed would continue when we were finished and my birthed challenged child would make sure of it and be protected and rewarded by Him.

 I could only say, 'Thank you, Aba.' Sam cried and Thanked GOD too. We slowly started hearing the ship sounds again with our moans not far behind. Sam was pumping so hard but light at the same time I couldn't hold myself anymore. I screamed that I loved him and loved him forever but asked him to stop. I was so tired my legs were numb and I couldn't move. He and his little friend were the only ones moving at this point. He told me he needed a little more time. He kept saying okay over and over. Then I almost passed out when he pulled back and not only rubbed my spot but it felt like it got licked. I felt him spray on it which made me scream with pleasure.

DAY EIGHT

We took our own suitcases off the ship. Since
we were considered VIP status we were among
the first people to debark the ship. We didn't
declare anything. I carried (5) Jamaican, (6)
Cayman and (8) Cozumel smokes. We walked
across the street to the parking garage,
loaded up and let the truck run for awhile
because it had been sitting for a week.
I asked Sam where we were going to spend
the night since we would be staying in Miami
that night. He said a condo. I asked whose
condo. He said his. I shook my head. I was
beginning to not be surprised.
He said we had to go to Tami-Ami airport to
pickup what Nan sent for me. It would be
waiting. We left the port and went to the
Tortuga building. All the employees knew Sam
and greeted him with hugs. He introduced me
as his lady.
There were six Octagon shaped, wood boxes.
Sam put them in the back after he let the
seat down. I asked for chocolate rum cake.
I was given a pan to take with us. We stayed
and Sam talked for awhile.

His plane was stored at this airport. He drove me over to see it. We boarded and I was so impressed. It was a jet that seated ten people. The seats were school colors. Okay I thought. Sam told me he had to go back to Cozumel in 2 or 3 weeks for a business meeting. He said he wanted me to go with him. I didn't answer. We left and went to his condo. It was near the downtown and beach area. It has a two car garage. We pulled into it. There was a brown car already parked inside. The door closed a dim light came on. We got out. We didn't take anything out of the truck initially. Sam went in first. He opened curtains to let natural light in. Once we took our suitcases out of the car, he showed me around. It was a 4 bedroom, brick which helped with the storms. It had storm windows and a deck. One bedroom had two beds. The 3rd room had a queen sized bed. The 2nd one had a desk with futon. We walked into the master bedroom. The bed was a king sized one and has yellow paisley covers with pillows. There is a chair by the window and TV on the wall. The closet is walk in. There weren't really many clothes hanging.

He said he's not there much but prefers his own space to a hotel. There was a hot tub on the deck. He had already had someone come by and prepare it, while we were on the cruise. He turned on some jazz music and I stretched out on the sofa. I asked him if I could smoke on the deck.

He said we can smoke in the house. I didn't wait for him to change his mind I pulled one of the joints from Cozumel. Sam lit his cigar. He said, 'Fro, I have a business, ball/meeting to go to tonight.'

I said, before he could ask that I can stay at the condo until he returns. He laughed out loud.

He wants me to come and wear Jacobs dress. I immediately said No! He asked why not. I said I didn't want to go to anymore business meetings on my vacation and I didn't know the people that would be there well enough to wear that dress. As a matter of fact I don't know what this is for. I thought. He said it's the coach's ball. He had to go if he ever wanted to be an NFL coach.

I looked over at him sitting in a lounge chair. All kinds of things were going thru my head.

Too many for him to answer! I remembered
what GOD said about standing up for him.
Was the goal to be an NFL coach his reward
and that's one of the reasons he needed me?
He answered without words, 'yes.'
He told me he's never taken anyone to the ball
and now people were talking about him and
making assumptions. He told his mentor last
year that he would be meeting me soon. They
don't believe him.
I went over and sat in his lap and hugged him.
I said, 'Okay, I'll go and wear the dress.' He
hugged and kissed me.
I told him I wanted to go out with him, on a
date without a meeting attached. He laughed
and asked if we can stay tomorrow night also.
I said yes.
He said he had the perfect spot and I don't
have to wear the dress there. I was happy to
hear this. We talked for some time and I
dozed off on the couch.
Sam woke me around 4pm. He was hungry.
We went to the garage and got in the brown
car which turns out to be my favorite color
and a Jaguar. I laughed so hard I almost
cried. He just shook his head.

We got fast food then came back to the condo to get dressed. I had already taken out my dress and the accessories and laid them on the bed. I couldn't help but think of Jacob. He was so blessed to do what he did and is doing now. If he had been a normal, physically fit man, the possibilities would be endless. I was becoming proud to help him by just wearing his style. I wondered what the ball/meeting was going to be like. I haven't been in a room full of that many men in a long time. I wondered how they will react to plain old me. I wasn't a diva, fashion model, rich or anything they were use to. I hope I don't make Sam look bad but they will certainly get a kick out of Jacobs dress. Sam came in the room and sat down on the bed.

He told me not to mention Jacob by name. They didn't need to know that yet. He said I could hold his hand if I was nervous when we got there, I was beautiful to him and that's all I should want to be, at least for tonight. Women would be there with their husbands, fathers and boyfriends. I asked him if Sara would be there.

He said he didn't know because he never expected her to be in Key Largo either. But either way, she won't want any trouble.

He said I was who he wanted and nobody else mattered. I liked the sound of that. I felt a little more at ease. Guess I have to get use to his world being so public.

He has done a wonderful job keeping so low key. I bet no one in that place could imagine who Sam really was. He smiled at me and said, 'you know.' We kissed and rubbed on each other for awhile then went to take a shower. It was nice but could not touch the bathroom in Cozumel.

I didn't take a shower with Sam. I used the tortoise cream and lotion from Nan. I didn't use the oil because I didn't want to overly attract any men. That dress was going to do what it do. My Mohawk was still hanging in there and really set the dress off nice. I put on lipstick and a little eye shadow. I really didn't like makeup because of having to remember to wash it off and I never liked the mess it seemed to make. Sam said without words, 'so that's your excuse, lazy! Its good God allowed your beauty.'

We left for the meeting/ball. We drove the Jaguar. It felt like I was a celebrity in that car. Sam had to know I really, really liked it, no loved it. He said without words, 'it's yours'. I said, 'stop playin'. He said 'this is my baby but I will take you over a car any day.' I reached over and kissed him. We finally got there and parked in Sam's first available as usual.

This man loved to take up front and first available parking.

People were piling in. It seemed to be only minorities. Sam said yes. I didn't know if I should feel happy or what. I didn't expect this. He said he would explain later.

We finally got out of the car and made it to the door before someone called out Sam's name. They called him Coach Max. An older man was behind us and Sam waited for him to catch up.

He smiled and shook his hand. He looked at me and smiled. He was with a light skinned, skinny woman. She was dressed nice but too skinny. She looked at the dress before she looked at my face. I couldn't tell what she was thinking by the look on her face.

He motioned to Sam who said, 'Oh, I'm sorry. Fro, this is Marcus Lee and his wife Shelia. Marcus is one of my mentors. This is my lady, Fro.

Marcus said, okay! Nice to meet you, Fro. Shelia shook my hand when I offered it. We all went inside. I felt like, oh my, what have I agreed to here. Sam squeezed my hand. He didn't let it go. I thought to myself, you better not leave me standing alone. I remembered what he did in Cozumel. He said without words, 'exactly'.

The deco in the foyer was very nice. We finally went into the large room with all the people mingling and music was playing. It seemed innocent enough. People looked at us but no one stared. We found our seats and sat down. A waitress came right over. I asked for a B&B and 7. Sam ordered a Henny and coke. Our drinks came pretty fast. I realized we were sitting at a table near the front.

Mr. & Mrs. Lee sat at the table next to ours. People were laughing and talking. Sam looked a little nervous. I said, 'baby, who are you looking for?

He said his primary mentor was Jerome Larkin. He is the master of ceremony.

I heard a sort of loud voice, it was coming our way. Sam's tension seemed to lessen. He sat back and I finally allowed him to release my hand. Jerome was headed straight for our table. He was with an attractive woman that looked mixed. She had on a high/low silk looking dress and heels. Her hair was hanging on her shoulders. He had on a black tuxedo similar to Sam's.

He said, 'there you are. I was looking for you man, thought you backed out on us.' Sam said, 'what's going on Jerome, they hugged and he said, 'Lynn, how are you?' He hugged her also. He turned to me, still sitting and said, 'baby, come over here!' He said, 'Fro, this is Jerome and Lynn Larkin.' His eyes went straight to my dress and then back up to my hair. He said, 'well, hello Fro."

Lynn offered her hand to me and looked at my dress also. She said, 'I love your dress.' I smiled and said thanks, I really like yours too. Jerome smiled hard at Sam. He told him, he didn't believe he would really bring a date this year. He told him that's good man.

I'm happy you found someone willing to spend time at an event like this with you. Sam laughed and said, 'what does that mean?' Jerome said, 'you know what it means!' You have never brought a date here. Not that one wasn't here for you already, but you never found anyone to come with you on your own! Lynn told him to stop teasing Sam. I looked at them and thought to myself, what the hell? I know this is not some sort of bet or some kind of freaky shit? Sam turned to me and said out loud, 'Jerome, Fro and I are dating. I love her and she loves me. She's the woman GOD sent to me and I'm keeping her, at all cost.' Jerome looked at me and smiled seductively. He asked me directly if Sam was telling the truth.

He said, 'Fro, how much did he pay you to come as his date? I will double the price if you tell me now.'

Lynn spoke up and told him that was a low blow and he better apologize right now. He said, 'No way! Sam knows the stakes and you mean all of a sudden he has a date but more over they are in love. He wasn't in love just 6 months ago!' Sam almost turned another color.

I could tell he had not expected the reaction.
He knew this may not go well for him, with me.
I was embarrassed. He didn't smile at all. He
tried to reach for my hand but I pulled back.
He said baby I'm sorry. He said he would not
have insisted I come if he had known I would
be treated with such disrespect by the men
he thought were his friends. A tear ran down
my face. I wiped it away.

Sam stepped toward me but I backed away. I
told him not to touch me. I looked at him
with, I'm sure, hurt in my eyes. I couldn't
believe this shit.

First his old girl calls me a bitch, than his boy
asked if I was a prostitute.

I didn't sign up for this shit. I knew this could
go one of two ways. I would cuss him and his
boi out, catch a cab and fly home tonight and
never answer his calls again and slap the shit
out of Jerome and Sam for allowing him to
speak to me that way. He doesn't know me
well enough to joke that way.

Or I could go to the bathroom and regroup
and teach them a lesson that they may or may
not get. I said, 'excuse me, 'and started to
walk off.

Sam caught me and said, 'baby I'm sorry, I didn't know.' I said loud enough for Jerome to hear me, 'I have to pee. I will be right back.' Sam said okay. I took 3 steps and looked back.

Sam and everyone near him including Jerome were watching me in that dress. At that moment I didn't care.

I found out where the bathroom was and made my way there. There were many women there. Checking their makeup, talking and laughing. They all looked at my dress and me when I walked through the door. I looked around like, 'and what?' I walked into an empty stale and pee'd. I cried for a couple of minutes, feeling like I was allowing myself to be made a fool of by Sam and his friends.

What kind of meeting was this anyway? Why does Sam want me to be here?

He's been wonderful to me but this doesn't feel good. I pinched my thigh til it hurt to see if I were dreaming. I wasn't. I stood against the stale door trying to decide how to handle this. Something, not Sam, said 'do you.'

Don't allow them to change you, you change them.

I was deep in thought when I heard someone call my name. It was Lynn. She knocked on the door. I said yes, what do you want? She said come out. I wiped my face and blew my nose. I walked pass her and went to a free sink to wash my hands. I splashed water on my face and pat it dry with a paper towel. Lynn watched me. I looked at her in the mirror.

She said I'm sorry my husband is such a jerk and was so rude to you. She said he has this thing with Sam that they need to keep private.

She looked at me closer and said, 'damn you not wearing any makeup.' I said, 'And?' She said and nothing. You are a beautiful, natural woman. No wonder Sam waited for you. I smiled at her. I told her I wasn't looking for him. He found me. She said he's been waiting for me for years. I asked her how she knew. She said he told her. Another woman co-signed. She said Sam refused to be with just any old woman.

Many women have tried to step to him but all were unsuccessful, including Michelle.

I asked who Michelle was. She said a spoiled woman who thinks because she has money from her rich father, she can have any man she wants even if he's taken.

She said Michelle is on her way to find you now. She wants to know who this woman is that Sam brought. She's crazy and I came to get you so she won't bother you. But I think you can hold your own. I said yes I can.

She said to come back because Sam is finished cussing out Jerome. He told Jerome if you leave him he's gonna beat Jerome's ass and he can do it too. We both laughed. I felt better talking with her. She asked about my dress. I told her I was wearing it for an up and coming designer from Jamaica.

It's called, 'Eternal Love'. She said it was gorgeous and I wore it well. I told her Sam insisted I wear it. She said he probably likes to look at my beautiful body in the dress. She said lets go.

Just then the door opened and I heard a woman talking loud. A tall, medium complexion, pretty woman walked in.

The other ladies stood around like they were waiting for a fight.

She looked at Lynn and then me. She asked
Lynn who was it in there that thought they
were dating her man. I sized her up and knew
I could take her if I had to.

I asked, before Lynn could answer, so who is
your man? She said his name is Sam Maxwell.
I walked right up to her. She backed up a
foot. I said, 'I don't know who you are and I
don't know what sick joke this is but I don't
play no childish or teenage games with nobody
about no man. I have a teenager at home.

She said Sam is always her date for this
event. I asked her, tell me, have you ever
been to his house, either of them, have you
ever met his family, gone on a cruise with him
and have you ever made love to or with him?
She said no but I can and I will.

I said, 'I have done all of that with him. We
are dating as of 4 days ago. I finally made up
my mind to accept him as my man. You and no
one else in here or anywhere else is ever going
to know him that way, again. If you don't
believe me, ask him yourself.

Let me tell you one more thing, I don't fight
over no man.

But if you step to me in my space and call me any name other than Fro, I will not hesitate to defend myself.' I tried to pass her but she wouldn't move. I pushed pass her. Lynn followed. I didn't look back.

I went back to the table, Sam stood up right away. He hugged and kissed me like no one else was in the room.

He said, 'baby, I love you. I really do. Don't leave me for anybody, I need you.

I smiled and said okay. I sat down beside Sam. I didn't look at Jerome. But I glanced at Lynn. She nodded yes and smiled. I smiled too. Jerome got up and stopped right in front of me. I looked at him wondering what he had to say now. Sam said without words, he does regret what he said. He wants to apologize, let him please. He picked up my hand and kissed it. He said, 'Fro, I apologize. I did not mean to offend you. I really thought this was a joke on Sam's part.

I guess I don't really know him as well as I thought but I would like to going forward, if you will allow it.

I'd like to get to know you also. He said he
knew I was not too receptive to him right now
but maybe in the near future.
I said, 'Ok, I'll think about it.'
He said, 'by the way thanks for not tagging
Michelle's ass. This event would have been
over before it starts.' I didn't respond.
He moved to the front podium and turned on
the microphone. 'Ok, I would like to call the
business portion of this meeting to order.'
He told everyone welcome, but he looked at
me. I put my head down. He continued his
welcome to the, 'Minority League of US
Coaches.' (MLUC) I had never heard of such
an organization.
He asked the treasurer to give a report.
Turns out he was Marcus Lee. He came up and
gave the report. He also told them a list was
in the corner of those who still had not paid
their dues for this year. He said they can pay
tonight or if any members in good standing
wanted to help, they could pay for them. He
yielded the floor back to Jerome after the
Treasurer report was accepted and a
2ndmotion was given.

Jerome talked about old business and went on to new business.

He said I make a motion to accept Coach Samuel Maxwell as our next project to push. He asked for a vote of yea and waited for nay. He said, so ordered.

I looked at Sam. He smiled hard. He got up and everybody clapped and cheered. Jerome said come on Sam. Give us a word or two. Sam grabbed my hand and squeezed it tight.

He stood up and walked to Jerome who gave him the microphone. He said I appreciate the support you have given me and are about to give. He went on to say he would never forget it and will do his part to support the next line. Lots of men cheered and got in a line to come shake his hand. I watched and smiled.

It was a blast to see him so happy. He was being accepted by his peers who had to also reach back and help.

If they only knew how much more advanced Sam was with this game than they are. Sam already does this as a business. Plus he has an advantage. One that they have no idea about! While that was happening I got up and got to the back of the line.

The ladies looked at me and most smiled. That dress was banging, my Mohawk was weathered and pretty.

I caught Michelle's eye. I saw her get up. I looked her right in her eyes and shook my head, No! She knew I meant it.

Lynn knew I meant it too. She stood up and started clapping for me. Other women stood and clapped also. The DJ played Alicia Keyes, Brand New Me. The guys were clapping too. I danced to myself as I moved up in line. A few guys dropped out of line.

The song came on again before I got to Sam. He smiled with his teeth showing.

I finally got to the head of the line.

I thought to myself, boi you are something else. What have I let you talk me into? What kind of ride is this? He held my hands with both of his, down low. He pulled them above and on his shoulders. He held me around my waist and pulled me to him. He said without words, 'ride or die baby.' I smiled. We hugged and rocked like we were dancing. We walked back to our seats.

Jerome said, 'alrighty then.' He said we have a tradition here and it has to keep going.

If you were invited by someone on the line you have to tell us who you are and answer two questions from the master of ceremony, me. We ordered another drink. I was not thinking that Sam was actually on the line, I listened but not closely. It looked like Jerome was picking on the visitors.

I was wondering when the music was gonna start. I wanted to dance. I wasn't wearing this dress anymore anytime soon and I wanted to get wear out of it.

Sam said without words, baby be good please. Before I could answer, Jerome walked over to our table and put his hand out to me. He said, 'it's your turn.'

I looked at Sam searching but he said, go ahead, only a few moments, and then we will dance. I looked around the room. The ladies were watching and so was Michelle. Lynn said, 'go on Fro, it's your turn.'

I gave Jerome my hand as he helped me up. There were 5 steps up to the stage with a microphone stand. He held my hand til I was almost up. Sam said, 'there goes my baby!' That made me smile.

I looked over the crowd. The men were shaking their heads and the women were admiring the dress and my shape in the dress. They were all surprised that Sam had it like that.

Jerome said okay before my questions, what's your name, what do you do and who invited you. I said my name is Frozine or Fro. Sam made me come. I am actually on vacation and didn't want to come. Now I'm glad I did, looking directly at Michelle. He said, 'what do you do and where are you from?' I'm from Va. Beach, VA and I work for the President of a major corporation. He said what do you do Fro? I make business decisions to help retain customers. I am an advocate.

So my questions are twofold. Are you and Sam really dating and when did this happen? Yes, Sam and I are dating. He's been pursuing me for a few months, we just came back from vacation in the Caribbean. I just made a decision a few days ago that I will date Sam. I didn't believe a fine man like him would want a woman like me. He said what do you mean a woman like you? I am not rich, fabulous and I don't act like so many others.

I'm just me. I can't pretend long, Jerome. My house is paid off, I have a high school senior coming up and I don't have a lot of patience to be played.

He said so you not with Sam for financial gain. I laughed out loud. What does Sam have to financially gain that you know about?

He said, 'Fro do you know what we do here?' I said No. He turned and looked at Sam. He said, 'man she doesn't know what this meeting is about?' Sam said, 'No, she doesn't.'

Jerome told me he had to ask for my forgiveness. I asked why. He said he thought Sam was teasing him and using me to do it. He said let me guess, you've been a PTA President haven't you? I bet it was a few years of it. I said yes! He said, 'your child, a daughter is in sports at school, a cheerleader? You want her to be stable so she can learn how to take care of herself? I said yes! He said, 'damn!'

I bet Sam has been working his ass off to convince you that he cares about you, and you are just beginning to trust him. Taking you out of town on vacation must have taken months. 'Yes'.

'Jerome, Sam and I bonded on an 8 day, 7 night cruise. GOD actually brought us together and turns out he is my soul mate or twin flame. I care about this man.' I looked at Sam and smiled. He nodded his head.
'It's hard standing here with you watching me in this dress. I'm shy! But I just have to take a moment to say I'm Sam's girlfriend and we are dating now. He is officially off the market for any women or men for that matter. I'm not sharing and neither is he, I looked at Jerome. An obsessive woman called me a bitch and she doesn't even know me, at all. What kind of immature shit is that? She doesn't even know Sam that well. But Lord have mercy, I do!' I fanned myself, I was getting hot.
Some guy yelled, I see you Ms. Fro! I looked toward the door. It was Cee. He said, 'whup whup.' I repeated to him. We laughed.
He said, ' y'all if it wasn't for Ms. Fro, I would have dropped out of school by now. She came to school to help me. I wouldn't let her meet Coach. I didn't know Coach was being run down by women he wasn't compatible with.

I think you two are meant to be together.
Coach, she go hard man! She be yelling at us
and talking crap when we lose and win. She
goes to all the games and read to me and let
me read to her. He's a good guy, Fro', Cee said.
Sam walked up to Cee and hugged him. 'We
saw the You Tube video', Cee said.
He said, 'we know you will probably lay hands
on some women who step to you wrong cause
ain't nobody got time for dat'. We all laughed.
Sam laughed and I did too.
I asked Jerome if he had any more questions.
He said No.
Sam came to the stage to help me down.
When I got to the last step he got in front of
me which made us face to face. We kissed
with tongues in each other's mouths. Sam put
his hands at the top of my hips. He touched
me like he was familiar with me.
Anyone with eyes would know this man is
sexing me up and we like it. We talked to Cee
for a little while longer and danced for a few
songs. We said goodnight to the mentors and
their wives. We left for the condo. I told
Sam I was tired. He said he was also. We
undressed and went to bed.

A DATE in MIAMI

We woke up early and went out to the hot tub. Before daylight! It was so nice to lounge and talk without words.

I took advantage and rubbed all over his little friend. We were gonna be real good friends. Even if Sam turned out to be a jerk I would refuse, he was gonna give me some of this. He was right. Once I got use to him I couldn't go back to anything else.

I hope he knows I have been letting him have his way without being lead by me. There are a few things I want to do to him too.

I have to admit he wore me out in that special shower. That man had him a good time. He knows he can tame my whole body. Sam pulled me to him. We kissed slowly and gently, he leaned me back and sucked my breast. I rubbed and pulled on his little friend, we both moaned with passion.

He stopped so we would slow down. I could go from zero to cruise in a few minutes.

He rubbed my back and it felt nice. He thanked me for not going all the way off last night.

He said he didn't stop anything but wanted to see how I handled things. He said it was a bit of a test. Especially the question and answer session. He said he had to see how I speak publicly and how I stand even in uncomfortable situations. He needed to know what training I would need.

He said baby THIS IS MY PROMISE. I always wanted to be an NFL coach.

But it doesn't matter how much money you have. You need people to support you. This group, mentors coaches! It works better if your personal needs are met. He said I was now a part of his world and it is different from the normal.

I agreed but I told him I can't change overnight. He put his finger over my mouth. He said, baby you are not understanding me. I love and want you just like you are.

Don't change, please don't change. I can't handle the other stuff. You know shaking and faking.

I said you sure you can handle me Sam? He laughed and said yes. We decided to stay in Miami one more day. He said we would go out tonight on a date. No meetings or anything.

I called to check on my teenager. She would be fine for a few more days.

I said yes. I wanted a real date. He said cool, let's go finish this in the house.

We went to his master and got back into bed. We made love a longtime, then took another nap.

We got dressed about 1 pm and went for a ride near the beach. It was nice spending time with Sam. He was funny and made me laugh. I made him laugh too.

I made him take photos of me posing beside the Jaguar holding up a sign that said I can have it. We had passerby's take photos of both of us beside the car. We went to a small park, he pushed me on the swing. He chased me, catching me every time. We sat in the grass he put his head in my lap for awhile then we switched. It was a nice ending to a special hard fought vacation resulting in love.

I totally didn't expect to be this vested in this man or any other man today. Sam told me to get use to it. He said he knew it was hard to adjust in such a short time. He said he was prepared to wait and give me time before more changes.

We left the park and headed back to the condo. It was beginning to get dark. We showered and dressed for a night out with just us in Miami. I wore a black dress that I didn't wear on the cruise.

With my stomach gone and my breast sitting high enough that no bra was needed I looked really sexy.

Sam wore a dark tan, linen blazer and chocolate slacks. He wore a white tee shirt. He was smoking hot. I told him, no wonder women had lost it over him.

He let it fall out of his mouth that he was a regular guy. I laughed out loud.

He quickly said ok. He said it's okay because all of that was behind him now. He doesn't have to pretend anymore. It was nice to be himself. I agreed with him. He is a sweetheart. We hugged and kissed for a few minutes before we left for dinner and dancing. We pulled in front of Shay's but Sam wouldn't let them valet. He said he would pay extra but they weren't getting in his Jag! They let him park up front with an extra tip. We got out of the car and went in. It was kind of dark but smelled very good. We had a front table.

I wore my ring, it glistened on my finger. Sam noticed it too. He smiled and took my hand. He said the ring was a very elegant design and he knew I would want it. He also said Fro, the ring is real. No 24kt or 10kt. It is a platinum design with real diamonds. He said the ring is valued at approximately $200k. I said, no way. He said, yes way. It's one of a kind so add $100k.

I told him all this time I thought it was a great fake. He said that would make him fake and he's not.

He said that this ring, he is considering as my engagement ring. I said okay! He kissed my hand.

We ordered food and drinks. He said there was going to be a celebrity guest. I asked who, he wouldn't say. He said it's a surprise. The dinner was good and hit the spot. Shortly after our plates were removed a lady came to the microphone and sang a song reminding me of Tyler Perry movie set with the dinner. I was so geeked. When she finished, the lights went down and Tamia started singing, Love, I'm Yours. I smiled so hard, my eyes filled with tears. He said, dance with me.

I stood up and he held me so special I shed a tear, Tamia smiled.

Wow, no one would believe all the things that have happened to me in a week. It seems like a dream even to me and I was there.

Does Sam really know who he has on his hands? He whispered to me that he knows me. I hugged him tight. He hugged me back.

Tamia came to our table after she sang one more song. She and Sam talked and laughed. Sam went to the bathroom and we spoke. She thanked me for loving her music and Sam. She said she's known him for years and he use to be lonely.

'I felt sorry for him but he had to wait like the rest of us. And look who he drew from the fountain of life. I'm quite taken with you. Your Mohawk is beautiful. The red streaks are awesome. Your lack of makeup speaks volumes. You look like the woman Sam would have chosen.

Are you happy Fro?' 'Yes, I am. I love Sam, I said. Still something off though. Why was I chosen? I'm sure there was another choice.'

'Unfortunately there wasn't', Tamia said.

She asked me if she can sing at our wedding. I told her that would be awhile. She said whenever it is she wants to sing for us. I told her yes. She smiled.

She asked how Sam was in bed. I told her words couldn't describe it. We satisfied each other beyond our expectations. I asked why she wanted to know. She said Sam told her once that no one could handle him. He was extra large.

'Well I guess we are compatible because no other man has ever been able to satisfy me before Sam. I have to say I'm thoroughly satisfied and so is he. If we weren't dating I would still want to be with him sexually.' She said, 'you nasty.' I said I know! We laughed! Sam walked up and said to me without words you are something else, Fro. I said what?, and smiled. He said, 'I told you don't do that!' 'Do what?' I said. 'Tell people about me', he said. 'So you're not sure if you can trust me now', I said.

Tamia interrupted and started talking.

I was so into Sam and my discussion, I almost forgot she was there.

Sam being the expert in relationships because of his advantage can multitask but I'm not an expert after only a few days and so I'm not taking blame for that. Besides I don't think I gave Sam advanced permission to include me. So homey better recognize. He must not know he actually has a diamond in the rough. So enjoy the blunders <u>now</u>.

I suppose he will revisit, '<u>now</u>' and remind me I'm not as good as he is. I can master talent too. I could take this speaking without words thing to a whole other level but I bet Sam knows that already.

He says out loud, 'Fro, stop being so shy in front of Tamia.' This snaps me out of my internal conversation with him. Okay! I refocus and tell Tamia that I do love her work and I'm actually blown away at this moment. Sam knows I will never forget this and I smiled at him.

She responded that's gotta be mind blowing but imagine how she feels knowing her friend Sam was lonely and found me and is very happy with his decision, to the point of cutting to the chase and introducing me to his friends, his close friends. You are indeed special.

You are the piece of him that's been missing.
From your own words he is that man.
Hey, I just want to **ride it til the wheels fall off**. The journey alone is priceless.
I stopped and held her hand, 'Stop woman! Stop writing another love song. I can hear it now...Ride it til the wheels fall off, in a song that you get an award for cause everybody will love it because they have felt or wanna feel that too.'
She said, 'touché' and laughed out loud. Sam told Tamia that's what he was talking about. She said, 'look! I'm always needing new material and you guys are my friends, right Fro?' She looked at me.
Okay, I guess we gotta support each other huh? She said, 'Sure you right!' I laughed at how down to earth she acted.
She said, 'Fro, it is truly an honor and my privilege to meet the sister that can handle this brother.'
She kissed me on my cheek and asked if it's okay if Sam gives her my telephone number. I said, 'Yes, of course'.

She got up and said she had to go. Sam said he'd be back he was going to walk Tamia to her car. I smiled and waved them off.

I had to pee but wanted another drink. I asked our waitress to bring me a White Russian with a side of Captain Morgan or Tortuga if they had it. She said, 'We have Tortuga miss. I said, "I will take Tortuga'. I asked her where the bathroom is before she walked off. She pointed, I left knowing she wouldn't put the drink on an empty table.

As I was going to the bathroom, I thought about Sam knowing he heard every word I said or thought. There seems to be a whole different layer to this man. Why is it he can get this kind of reaction from people, places and things that I like. He seems to know me way too well.

Nan and Poppy must be making a killing with the import of rum to the US. Why are these people Sam's relatives and love me already. I love them too. But I loved their products years ago. How did that happen? He knew I would accept Jacob as he is and we'd learn to love and trust each other. I can't give these people back to Sam with no contact.

That door is opened and Sam had no power to close it.

When I got back to the table Sam was seated and my drink was waiting. He stood up when I got to the table because he was sitting in my seat when we had company at the table.

He held the chair out for me and pushed me close to his chair before he sat in it.

I laughed out loud. He smiled seductively.

The waitress brought him his drink. We both took a long swallow and put the drinks down.

He reached over and gave me a long, slow kiss. He held my chair on the sides and rubbed my hips with his thumbs only. It was so ticklish I almost squirmed.

He sat back and looked at me. He didn't speak for almost a minute. I thought to myself he must need me to press his reset button. He laughed now so I know he heard me.

He said he had a question that only required a yes or no answer. I nodded.

He said, 'I'm not going to be able to get you to do what I say, am I?' I said no, not everything. 'You will probably be able to master your gifts and the knowledge of mine before very long.' I said, 'yep'.

He knew these things but had to hear me say it. He said, 'Fro, I know you didn't ask for it but you are now a part of my family and I yours. I can't give you back. I need everything you are now and will be, to move forward with my life. You have to admit you need me too. Yeah, I said I did need our relationship but if he turned out to be a jerk, I would go to plan B. He reached over and ran his hand down my Mohawk. He said, this hair is beautiful and fits you. Too bad you don't have to think about any plans. I have adjustments to make too. I won't pick petty battles, Fro. You must know that. I reached over and ran my finger from his forehead to his chest. He closed his eyes and smiled. I kissed his forehead. I moved back to drink my White Russian. He asked me if I understood better now. He said, 'Fro, my contacts are long. Most people don't know me but now they will because they will be interested in you. You don't fit their typical profile. They don't want to tangle with you but then again they do and will want to summarize their interaction with Sam's woman.

They will be afraid of crossing you or being in your business too much.

You could do the same to them, on a personal or professional level. They would know if they cross the line in your life without your consent they will have to go to court for a charge or watch their personal backs.

It wouldn't take but one interview for them to know the rules and consequences for breaking them. I need that umbrella too. I want to be able to take care of my back and be focused on the task at hand. You are here to be part of my back, and I yours.

Our personal needs are met and they aren't going to change with the weather. So that leaves life and our calling. You know mine Fro he said.

I told him I still had questions no matter how he tried to smooth it over. He rubbed my arm and ran his hand up my arm to my shoulder and to my chest. He traced my cleavage with his finger. My nipples started getting hard. He saw it. He said baby your body is so receptive to me. I said I know and that's a problem, he said no it wasn't because he can handle whatever rises. I said okay Mr. Maxwell.

He told me I can't have any doubts after what we've experienced. I had to agree with him. As if on cue, Tamia's song, 'you put a move on my heart', came on. He got up and pulled me up. I shook my head and smiled hard. We were a step from the dance floor. I walked around the table and backed up on the dance floor, swaying as I moved back.

He walked up to me and held my hand turning me around full circle and shaking his head, smiling with a look on his face I haven't seen before. He oozed swagger.

I could only respond. He held me in his arms and we swayed in rhythm. It was unbelievable the vibe that went through me at that moment. He swayed and I followed.

It felt like we were making love on the dance floor. I said what the hell and let go of my shyness for that moment.

He put his hands on the top of my behind and guided me into him, back and forth. I rubbed my chest into his with firm strokes. I put my arms up around his neck, and held on. It was an adventure. Sam could dance, really dance.

He said without words, this is what I want to do to you right now. You have me twisted up in the game, Fro,' he said. I was so overwhelmed with emotion I couldn't speak.

He pushed away from me and I kept the same steps on my own, so did Sam. When the song was over, he pulled me to him and kissed me with power and passion. That combination was a bit thuggish.

We walked back to our seats. We were unaware of the people still in their seats watching us. I/We didn't care.

He asked if I was ready to go. I said I guess you are? He said he wanted a chance to love me right. I told him he has many times. He said, no, not like this.

You probably can't take me right now, I'm feeling very intense. He put his hand on my knee and squeezed. He wanted me right now and I knew it.

He looked over at the manager and the manager shook his head yes. Sam said come on Fro, I want to show you something. We got up and walked back pass the bathrooms and around the corner. He opened the door.

The manager's office was very nice. He held my hand and walked through a door at the back of the office. It was a small lounge room. He locked the door. He pulled my dress above my head and laid it on the chair, he pulled his jacket and pants off too. Then his t-shirt. His little friend was a step ahead. I pulled my panties off before they got soaking wet. He pulled a single chair from a table nearby and sat it in the middle of the room. He pulled me to him. I pulled his underwear down being careful not to hurt his little friend.

I bent down in front of him and put the head in my mouth. I held the rest of him in my hands. I got on my knees and sucked as much as I could. Then I took him out and licked him to the base. I blew and sucked all the way back to the tip. Sam closed his eyes, put his head back and asked me to do that again. He held onto my hair.

This time when I put the head in and started to suck he moved back and forth and held my hair and said suck it like a popsicle. I did. He moaned with pleasure and said, damn baby, you mean I been missing this feeling.

Nobody has ever made love to my erect little friend. Stop baby, that's enough. I can't take it. I said no, between sucks.

I went back down to the base with licks, he moaned. I picked up his balls and licked one and then the other he started backing up. I pulled him back to me without releasing and sucked one in my mouth, he gave out a light scream.

I said to myself be still baby, I won't hurt you. He said, 'what?' He was out of it. I released that one and sucked in the other one. He said oh my GOD baby what are ... and a moan of pleasure left his mouth when I rubbed the back of his little friends head with my other hand. I ran my tongue around the ball and he continued to moan in pleasure. He kept trying to say stop. I released him and sucked and licked my way back to the tip. I kissed the head and stood up.

He said, Damn! He came close to me and kissed my mouth. He wanted to know what he tasted like too. He kissed me as he went down and opened my thighs.

He licked, sucked and swallowed all of my juices he came in contact with. He did not stick his tongue inside her.

He got over to the chair and sat down. He pulled me to face him. I sat on his little friend which slid right into my wetness.

I fell into Sam's arms. He held, kissed and fucked me til I came and then laid on my spot so I was still having an orgasm when he came. I felt it spray inside me. He repeated the slowing down of our actions til he was softer. We kissed long and hard while this was happening.

I got up, found paper towels from the bathroom near us and wiped the juice off me and gave Sam one to do the same.

I went in the bathroom to allow the bulk of this juice to drop in the toilet. It did too. I wiped off, washed my hands and rinsed my mouth before leaving the bathroom. Sam did the same thing. We put our clothes back on and straightened up and left the office.

That was so intense. I never meant to show him my hand. The opportunity could not be avoided. He looked at me with a grin on his face.

We stopped at the bar to get one last drink before leaving. There were no drinks at the condo. The manager asked Sam if everything was okay. Sam said, 'yo man, good looking out.' He paid the check, left a tip with the manager and waitress. He also tipped the parking attendant. The car was still in the same place and in tack. The drive back to the condo was quiet except Sam made a lot of noises and shook his head a lot.

When we pulled into the garage and the door closed, I said, 'Sam, don't sleep on me either.' He looked at me and said he won't.

We got out of our clothes and prepared our suitcases to be put in the truck. We took out riding clothes. I wore a long skirt and matching top. Sam wore non wrinkled pants and a button down shirt.

I found a joint and Sam found his cigar. We went out on the deck to smoke this time. We hugged a lot and kissed softly.

We went back inside and looked at the weather channel before turning off the light. Sam found my soft spot and gently rubbed it. It started getting wet. He turned me over and took me from the back. It was so good.

You Knew Me! The Truth Revealed

We have officially been together for 10 straight days. I haven't been with a man this way since my husband died.

It's something else, this life we live. We can make all the plans we want to but ultimately when there is a calling on your life, your plans are not your plans, they're HIS plans. You have a timetable or a plan for yourself but when HE wants you to do something, your plans can instantly become HIS plans.

There was no preplan for Sam to be in my life. I was comfortable in my little city, helping my youngest of three children spread her wings. That is my debt to her. I could have delayed meeting Sam for another year but no, HIS plan was for us to meet now. I'm really feeling this man. I certainly can't deny that but this still feels bigger than what I see.

All of this was on my mind before 6am. Was hoping I didn't wake Sam, he had to drive. I slipped out of bed for a hot shower. I used the oil. Sam had been working her out. I have never had sex like that for 10 straight days.

I felt refreshed when I stepped out of the shower. Just then Sam stepped in the bathroom. I started putting on lotion. Sam reached for my hand. He guided me back to bed. He said he wasn't finished. I pretended to fight him off when he opened my thighs and started over again. What a fruitful hour!

We were back on Hwy 95 North. Sam drove through Florida (FL). I started driving in Georgia (GA). I asked him if I could stop in South Carolina (SC) to speak with my mom. It felt like he knew we would go.

I wanted to put flowers on my people's graves. He was good with this. We stopped at a roadside store to get 25 or 30 bushes of flowers.

We arrived in SC and went straight to the graveyard. Didn't want to get tied up with people and forget or it get too late to go to the graveyard.

I introduced him to the characters that helped build me to the person I am now. The people I really loved the most and loved me are buried here. I told Sam this is where I want to be buried when I die. He said ok, then asked if I mind if he's buried in Jamaica near his mom. I told him if I out live him, I will make sure of it. As we were finishing up, the Pastor drove up. He came over to speak with us. I told him who I was and introduced Sam. He seemed to be a little troubled.

Sam said without words that we should go back to his office with him for a minute. I asked the Pastor if we could speak with him for a moment in his office. He agreed. Sam got straight to the point. He asked the Pastor why he was troubled.

He told us that the majority of the members were older and couldn't continue to financially support the church. He was having to look at alternatives like selling property, but knew the members would have a fit.

I asked him how much remained on the mortgage. He said (1) million. There was property they wanted to buy but can't. I thought to myself, we could help but I hate asking my new boyfriend for money that large. Sam said, Pastor, if you didn't have a mortgage and had the land you wanted paid off, with a little money in the church account to help the people, would this ease your burden? He said of course but no one who's a member has that kind of money. Sam left the office saying he would be right back. I told the Pastor I wanted to pay for a few plots for me and my children. He said it was $300.00 each.
I told him I would pay $500.00 each.
I gave him instructions about where I wanted the plots and wrote him a check for $2000.00 for all of us. He said he would have a receipt and instructions mailed to me or he would give it to my mom.
Sam came back in with his briefcase. He pulled out a business check book. They went over the details of the mortgage balance, insurance and cost of the additional land. Sam wrote him a check for (2) million.

The Pastor sat back in his chair and tears filled his eyes. They started falling on his clothes. He got up and started shouting. He thanked GOD for Favor and sending an angel in his time of distress. He said he would be a good steward of the money and make sure all needed details were completed. The mortgage would be paid this week, land will be acquired and he won't even take up collection for the rest of the month.

He would suggest members pay some of their own debts and wants and help someone else. That's what Jesus would do. He thanked us again before we left and hugged us tight. He told us to take care of each other. We promised we would. We felt light when we left the church office. I stopped to visit a few other relatives in the area before we went to see my mom. She was happy to see us. She asked Sam a lot of questions including what his intentions were for her daughter. My mom must have forgotten I was grown. We listened to her talk and Sam laughed a lot. He told her I was harder on him than she was. She told him that's how I grew up and it was too late to change now. He laughed.

He asked her if she needed anything. She said no, but she wanted to see her grand children and great grands more.

He told her maybe we could all take vacation together for a week. She could get her fill of them and then send them back home. She laughed and said that would be nice.

We prayed together and I was careful not to pray for a compete healing of an 80 year old. She wouldn't want to outlive all of her relatives and friends.

We told her we weren't staying because my daughter was expecting us the next day and Sam had to get back to work.

My mom called me by my nickname and I should have known Sam wouldn't miss it. He asked me to let him drive. He had one more stop to make. I wondered who he knew in my home town. He said without words, that I would soon find out. He drove in the direction of my cousin's church.

It was approx. 7 pm so they would probably be having their Sunday evening service.

I laughed to myself thinking this is how this man knew so much about me.

My cousin told him. I was floored. Sam didn't say a word. He kept smiling. He got a phone call and I heard him say, 'she doesn't know yet.' He said, 'okay' and hung up. We pulled in front of the church. There was someone who directed him to park up front in the Pastor's space. I just shook my head. We weren't dressed up but okay for a night service.

We were escorted in by one of my younger cousins. I hit him in the chest and asked what this was about? He held his chest and laughed. We went into my cousin's office. He came in and he and Sam hugged like they were boi's forever. I shook my head. My cousin pulled me to him and held me in an embrace that said he loved me but gotcha!

He called me by my nickname too. He asked me to allow him to explain before I got mad. I crossed my arms wondering what he has done, and if I would get the truth. He told me to sit. I did.

Sam stood and leaned on the wall near the door. My cousin, the Pastor began by saying that he met Sam in college and they have been friends for years.

He said he knew Sam was lonely and waiting for GOD's plan to unfold for his life. Sam recently came to him with two pictures he took of a woman he thought was the one but he couldn't find her.

Sam showed him the first picture, he laughed but when he showed him the second picture he fell on the floor and laughed.

He asked Sam how he knew this woman was her. Sam didn't know, he just had a feeling. He said he told Sam this was his cousin, Fro. I was something else and would not make it easy for Sam if he had any odd stuff going on. He told Sam about me because I was his cousin who he knew but Sam was his good friend who he had come to know.

He knew Sam wouldn't hurt me and knew Sam needed someone who didn't take much shit and would fight if necessary for what they believed in. He grew up with me and knew this about me.

He said he warned Sam that I wouldn't just take anything he said and believe him. He told Sam I was nice but stubborn and loved hard when I did.

My husband hadn't been gone that long and I may not be interested in a relationship right now.

He also told Sam if he could convince me, he would have a ride or die chick forever. He said he made a wager with Sam. If he could convince you to date him I would support his mission to become an NFL coach. He's wanted to do that as long as I've known him.

He needs his house in order first. He needed to be satisfied, feel safe, be able to trust a woman to hold him down and not have to worry about allegations of wrong doing with other women or men for that matter.

He told Sam that he knew me from childhood and even though he didn't know all I was doing, he knew I came from excellent stock and would suit Sam's needs if he could convince me. So has he?

I held my head down smiling in disbelief. This man has known about me all along and didn't let on a word about it.

I should put him on punishment but I will be punishing me too. Has he been playing me all along?

Does he really love me for me or does he just need me for my skill set.

Wait a minute! GOD spoke with us!

I looked at Sam who looked scared of my reaction and my cousin waiting to see if I was gonna cuss him out.

He knew I could and would and go tell his mom, also my cousin who I loved like my own mom. I stood up and said, 'Okay! Yes, he convinced me. He actually did more.

He introduced me to his family and I could really grow to love them. Kind of do already. I don't want to give them back.' My cousin said he told Sam that I wouldn't be afraid of his handicap relative.

'So cousin you all having service or a concert?' He said both. I asked him was it being recorded for radio. He said yes!

Sam interrupted and said good, find a place for me to speak for a few moments.' He had his briefcase with him.

My cousin said, sure. I'm thinking to myself you gonna let Sam speak to your people, you must trust him. Then again, you trusted him with me. I told my cousin I guess I will continue speaking to him.

But he should have told me. He said he was more concerned about what I would do to Sam than the other way around. I hit him in the chest also. We all walked out of his office and into the sanctuary. I held Sam's hand. He squeezed mine. They had saved a seat for us up front.

Almost no one knew me with my new hair style and I don't think they knew Sam by the stares we received.

I spoke to a few of my other cousins I saw. They knew who I was anywhere no matter what hair I had.

When the song and prayer were over, the Pastor said, 'I want to ask you to allow a few minutes for a good friend to speak.' He motioned to Sam. He stood up and turned around to face everyone. He told them that he was a child of the King and has always known it.

He told us he met the Pastor in college and have been friends ever since.

He recently met the Pastors cousin who some of them probably know, Fro or my nickname, some people shook their heads yeah because they knew me by my nickname.

He told them I was born and raised for him. I was his soul mate and vice versa.

He couldn't Thank GOD enough for his blessings but of course wondered what took so long.

He said sometimes we have to wait until it's our time. It doesn't always work out well if it's not our time. There were a lot of Amen's heard. He said, 'I want to be a blessing to this body. I am not a robber or thief. I am a coach and business man.' He opened his briefcase and took out two checks. He held up one and looked at my cousin, the Pastor.

He said, 'Pastor how much is remaining on the mortgage balance for this church?' Pastor was surprised by the question but said 2.1 million. He said, 'Sam you not going out telling our business are you? Sam, laughed.

He held up the first check again and said, 'I want to donate 2.5 million to pay off your mortgage.' There was a hush all over the church. Sam held up the other check and asked me to come to him. He spoke without words telling me to say what my mom's Pastor said about no tithes or offerings for a month.

I got up and took the check from Sam. He held my other hand. I said, 'you all know I love you even though I no longer live here. I was baptized at this church years ago.

I want to ask my cousin to do this that I'm about to ask without question or push back. I looked at my cousin with a look that said you owe me. He said, 'okay', out loud. I looked at the check and looked at Sam. He shook his head yes.

I said, 'we are asking you to not pay tithes or offerings for the rest of this month.' Quiet fell as they looked at each other. 'We are asking you in Jesus name to pay yourself debt free or help someone you've always wanted to help. Do something for yourselves you've always wanted to.' Sam said to me without words, 'we, baby.'

I said, 'we are interceding on your behalf. We will pay your tithes and offering for the rest of this month by offering $500k. to cover you.'

Another hush went through the sanctuary. I said, 'this should include those of you singing and from another church.'

They yelled and broke out into a shout. The whole church was shouting. This included my cousin, the Pastor.

His mom caught my eye and waved me over to her. She hugged me tight and told me she loved me always and knew I would bring her joy one day, like this. She said her husband knew too. He told her so before he died. I started shouting too.

I felt so overwhelmed because I loved my cousin's father like the father I never knew as a teenager. He was always so loving to me, even though his wife was my blood cousin. I passed out, slain in the spirit. While unconscious, I heard the still, small, powerful voice say,

'Good, my sweet girl. Your obedience has and will continue to be rewarded.'

I knew it was GOD speaking to me. 'I asked was it true? Is Sam sent from him?'

HE said, 'yes my child'.

I felt me coming back to myself. I was sitting, leaning on my cousin's mom's shoulder. She was rubbing my arm and crying. I hugged and kissed her. I whispered that I will see her again soon. She said okay.

I got up and went back to Sam and hugged him. He held me tight. I wanted to kiss him but knew they wouldn't understand. He gave me a quick kiss on my lips. I was compelled to go to the organist and asked him to play Yolanda Adam's song, 'Be Blessed.' He laughed because he said they practiced that yesterday. He said the person singing it couldn't be there so they weren't gonna play it. He said, 'Will you sing it?' I said yes. He was happy.

People were calming down he played the start of the song twice.

Sam said without words, 'I know you can do this baby.' The organist started a 3rd time. I started singing and the whole church felt it. I don't know how I knew the words, all of them. It sounded like I'd been singing for years. The organist was playing and swaying. Sam smiled and so did my cousin, the Pastor. When I looked at the faces of the people, they were crying and shaking their heads in agreement. When the song was over, they stood up and applauded. I shouted, 'Thank you GOD' over and over.

Sam held my hand tight and smiled at me. He said out loud, 'You are the whole package, Fro. Now you know why I want you and why I couldn't tell you everything. GOD had a surprise for you. I am an obedient man when it comes to the one that keeps us, Our Father!' I smiled and realized at that moment I was his and he was mine.

We would do our jobs well for the LORD and we were being rewarded at the same time. Nobody but GOD could have pulled this off. I was happy to be played by HIM!

We got up and went outside and my cousin followed knowing Sam was parked in his space. He hugged Sam and said welcome to my family man.

He hugged and kissed me and told me he loved me and I couldn't have made a better choice than allowing Sam to love me. He was the TRUTH! But so was I!

We all laughed. Sam and I got into the truck and got back on the highway for home, in VA. We were so full, we didn't speak for awhile. After we were back on I95, we talked and laughed. We drove all night but it wasn't hard.

We got on the final leg to Va. Beach and I took over driving. Sam was asleep by the time I pulled up to my house.

I sat there Thanking GOD for this traveling mercy and for my new life that was just beginning again.

No one would believe this was the truth but I knew it was. I could finally say, 'Yes, Sam is the Truth.'

****

THE WHOLE PACKAGE II

Sam would be leaving to go home to his house in Charlottesville. It is a 2.5 hour drive. He helped carry the crates inside and through the house to the back yard. We took all of my things out of the truck so they wouldn't be left in the heat.

Sam wanted to go upstairs to rest before his trip home after dinner. My youngest wasn't home yet. I was a little nervous because I had not had another man in my bedroom. I believe Sam is marking his ground. I had already replaced the bed. I did promise to date him. We took off our clothes and got into bed. Without my help, Sam made love to me. He was good at controlling my body's reaction to him.
...to be continued

Acknowledgements

To GOD, the Creator of Heaven & Earth and everything in it, I give ALL Honor and Glory because I never knew I could write continuous thought. Every time I found reason's to quit, you literally removed my excuses.

To Jackie aka Lisa who pushed and challenged me after President Obama was sworn in for the second time. We were there as witnesses on my birthday. You inspired me. This journey would not be the same without you.
To my Family for your prayers and patience with me cause GOD is not finished with me yet.
To my Friends who paid me in advance for this read, the last leg of a project always seems hardest. You encouraged me to keep going to the end. You all are a blessing. I desire to be the same to you.
To my Haters who's attempts to discourage me by giving negative criticism with no positive follow up. It didn't work. What you meant for my bad was used for my good. Attempting to kill anyone's dream will never be a part of my life.
Last but **NEVER** least my husband Craig, you believe in my dream and have shown you believe in me. Words can't express my gratitude. I will always Love You!

Sincerely,
Frozine

DO YOU WANT TO EARN $200 CASH?

Here's how it works.
There will be a reprint of this book.
I would like an **UPGRADED** front cover.
If you, the reader or someone you know, wants
or needs to **earn $200.00 CASH,**
(NO money orders check card, check, etc.)
Contact me at the email address below and
send me your draft cover idea. Deadlines will
be advised through initial email response.
If I agree...
I will pay **$100.00 plus $25.00 tip.**
There is a sequel coming out later this year.
It also needs a front cover.
I will pay another **$100.00 plus $25.00 tip.**
You will be acknowledged in both the reprint
and sequel.

COVERS_FRO@COX.NET

www.ingramcontent.com/pod-product-compliance
Lightning Source LLC
Chambersburg PA
CBHW031111030726
47496CB00002BA/489